TIME PORTAL

Ross Richdale

When Rhett intercepts a stranger, Shelley in his holiday home it becomes apparent that she is not just an intruder caught in the act of illegally trespassing.

Rhett and Shelley travel through a space-time portal where they are met by Dee, their twelve-year old daughter that they never knew existed. Dee is desperate for her brother, Corwin to be rescued. He has been caught in a trap set by the girifa, the reptilian equivalent of humanity. In this world, humans are the aliens.

As they continue their journey they befriend fellow travellers, who help them in a seemingly haphazard quest. However, their lives appear to have been predetermined with a destiny that will affect not only present day Earth but also the future.

Evil forces are also out there with sinister objectives of their own. Rhett and Shelley learn that the enemy are not the girifa but humans living a parallel world from their ancestors' time.

But who is really in control? Journey through the time portal where time, space and parallel worlds intertwine with an ultimate disaster that only Rhett and Shelley can halt.

PURRBOOKS

National Library of New Zealand Cataloguing-in-Publication Data

Richdale, Ross, 1941
Time portal / Ross Richdale.
ISBN 978-1-877438-22-6
I. Title.
NZ823.3—dc 22

Cover design by Ross Richdale

Paperback published by

Purrbooks
Palmerston North
NEW ZEALAND

CHAPTER ONE

He sat straddling the roof of the holiday home and wiped perspiration from his brow. January, high summer in the southern hemisphere, was hot. It almost too hot now for the iron on the roof reflected the overhead sun. This made his job almost impossible. Perhaps he should stop and come back up in the cool of the evening.

No, he'd try it one last time to align the satellite dish so they could receive all the television channels rather than just two available a Riversdale, the remote beach resort tucked in behind hills away from any television transmission tower. His sister, Val had told him it was false economy purchasing the cheap unofficial box and dish, as they had to be manually aligned. Perhaps she was right. The references in the manual were vague, too with the only grid reference being to Masterton, the closest large town, fifty kilometres away.

"Uncle Rhett," the girl shouted up from the lawn below. "It's almost working. Mum said to twist it back a little."

"Right Ava," Rhett called back.

He reached out with his fingers to rotate the screw clockwise a few millimetres. When he touched the hot metal an electric shock jolted him. He jerked back in alarm and shook his head. A sphere of energy the size of a tennis ball sat on his opened hand. It tickled rather than repeated the electric shock before it lifted, floated away like a bubble and disappeared in the sunlight.

Rhett Pennant frowned and stared out across the lawn. He could see the local road with holidaymakers walking along in beach attire, the usual quad bikes that seemed to be a necessity in the village and the neighbour's cat sitting in shade under a bush. The spark or whatever it was had gone.

"Uncle Rhett," Ava screamed with alarm in her voice. "What did you do?"

"Did you see something, too?"

"A yellow fireball came out of your hand. Are you okay?"

"Got a kick back from the dish. You'd better ask your mother to turn off the tellie."

Ava turned. "Mum," she screamed. "Uncle Rhett wants you to turn the tellie off. He got a shock."

Val appeared and glanced up. "You be careful, Rhett," she called out. "Just leave it. We can get a service man in next week."

"And pay a hundred bucks travelling expenses. No, toss me one of those rubber gloves you use for painting and I'll have one last try."

"Okay, but it is foolish to play with live wires. I'm leaving everything off."

Rhett smiled. His sister and brother-in-law had taken him under their wing since Lesley; his wife had died the winter before. It had been a difficult time but he was mainly over it now and could see a way forward in his life. He slipped on the gloves Val tossed up and reached out, somewhat apprehensively, to touch the screw. There was no shock so he twisted it a fraction.

It took several adjustments by trial and error for Val refused to turn the set below back on until his hands were away from the dish. Finally, though, he heard a scream of delight and five-year-old Kristine ran out.

"It works Uncle Rhett," she screamed as she jumped up and down in delight. "We've got the cartoons."

"But not for long," Ava cut in as she, too appeared on the lawn. "I want to watch C4."

This was a music channel that seemed to be mandatory viewing for local New Zealand teenagers. Rhett grinned for Ava was only eleven. They grew up so quickly in this modern age.

*

"Why don't you come back with us, tomorrow?" Rhett's brother-in-law Jerry Antworth said that evening.

Rhett shrugged for he knew he'd miss the family. "No, I've still got a week's holiday and I want to get the front deck painted."

Val and he had inherited the holiday home half way along Blue Pacific Parade and had joint ownership. It was an excellent arrangement with Val's family using it more than himself. He sighed, for the family he'd always wanted had never eventuated with Lesley's illness becoming progressively worse over the eighteen months before her death.

Val smiled. "You know we're only going back because the girls start school on Tuesday." She turned to Jerry. "And you have to pick them up, My Dear."

Rhett glanced up. Val and Jerry's girls were a delight. Back in Wellington where they all lived, he saw them often and helped whenever he could. His position as an electronics technician with a local firm involved night work so he was free several times a week to pick the girls up from their local primary school, now that Val had returned to full time employment.

Jerry rubbed his chin. "Yes, it would be a good idea for you to return today, Rhett. It's quite a rush for me trying to get to the school by three." He ducked away as Val gave him a dig in the arm and broke into a grin. "Okay, I know but they could take the bus home."

"Dad!" Ava cried.

"I'll be fine," Rhett said. "I'll get the deck done and I want to get those shrubs out the back trimmed too."

"And get onto Ellen, the cleaning lady," Val continued. "She does a good job cleaning after tenants have left but has the habit of..." The conversation continued as usual before the girls drifted off to see the new channels coming in and the adults cleaned up. Rhett watched the cars vans and trailers travelling on the road outside.

There was almost a mass exodus and Rhett knew that the hordes of children and teenagers were heading home to begin a new year at their schools. By Tuesday, peace would return to the village with the mainly elderly permanent residents able to reclaim their turf. He wondered what the new year would bring.

*

By nine the following morning the family had gone. Rhett glanced around the living room. It was funny how a place seemed to change when it was empty. He smiled when he realised Val had even washed the breakfast dishes and tidied the rooms. The washing machine hummed away, washing the sheets and other attire.

He didn't feel like painting yet so wandered across the road, through a right-of-way and over a small sand hill. Ahead was a view he'd seen a thousand times before but still loved. The tide was half way in with a row of breakers curling over and crashing down. Surf ran up the sand before retreating back to meet the next wave. To his right, the bay curved away to a flat topped hill while, in the opposite direction was the main bathing area and surf club buildings beside a small river, after which the village was named.

Further north again the beach ended in a rocky outcrop that extended up the coast to Castlepoint, the next settlement where a lighthouse clung to a rocky point.

"Hi Rhett," a voice behind him said. "Family gone, I see,"

He turned and grinned. Old Matthew was a local identity and would be eighty or more. But he still had a swim every day during the summer and was now standing in his swimming trunks with a towel draped around his leathery shoulders.

"Oh hi, Matthew," Rhett replied. "Yeah, school starts. I'm staying on a few days to get the deck painted."

"Want a hand?"

"Love one. I thought I'd leave it until later in the afternoon when the deck's shaded. About four."

"Sure," Matthew said. "Did you hear the latest?'

Rhett grinned. If there was any gossip around, Matthew picked it up.

"Everyone's leaving?"

"Not only that but some young lass was seen skinny dipping and then she had the audacity to steal clothes off the Smith's clothes line. Know them, the family three up from you with that tribe of kids?'

Rhett didn't but let the old guy ramble on. Most locals were quite honest with very little pilfering taking place in the village. Also, skinny-dipping that Matthew called nude swimming was unusual in this small conservative community.

"Seems she just stole Pauline Smith's clothes and a towel. Nothing else. They saw her disappearing through their back gate, still in the nude and running like a greyhound. A few others saw her heading back over the sand hills to the beach here." Matthew chucked. "Missed seeing her myself, unfortunately."

Rhett frowned. He should be mystified about this small incident but strangely, he wasn't. It was as if he had expected it to happen.

Matthew raised his eyebrows. "You saw her too?"

"No such luck." Rhett laughed and changed the topic of conversation. They chattered for a while before Matthew headed away.

Rhett spent an hour just wandering along the beach before he visited the local shop, bought a few groceries and went home.

Standing in his kitchen munching a sandwich and holding a mug of steaming coffee was a woman probably in her late twenties She was slim, wore a white top, a denim skirt and yellow jandals, the sandals that one poked toes through. Long dark hair hung down to her shoulders. More unusual in that first impression was that her skin was pale, not tanned as nearly everyone in the village was after a long hot summer.

"What the..." Rhett gasped. "What are you doing in my house, madam? I would advise..." He stopped when the woman's eyes caught his.

Her lips quivered and quite unexpectedly, tears flooded her eyes. Huge drops slid down her cheeks and dropped unhindered onto her top. She placed the half eaten sandwich down and grasped a chair with shaking hands.

"There's nobody else and I know I can trust you, Rhett," she sobbed. "Please, listen to me."

Her English sounded educated and had not a trace of an accent. Obviously, she was a typical New Zealander. But Rhett knew that she wasn't. He didn't even know why he knew. He just did.

"Okay, sit down and finish your coffee... err..."

"You know my name, Rhett Pennant."

Rhett gasped for he did. "Shelley Medina but how could I? I have never met or even heard of you before?'

The girl wiped the tears from her face and smiled almost shyly. "I implanted my name in your mind when I extracted yours. But call me Shelley."

"Oh sure," Rhett felt annoyed.

"How's your hand, Rhett?"

Rhett glanced down at the small blister in his right palm caused by the fireball. It still smarted a little when he used it.

"You?" he gasped.

Shelley nodded. "I homed in on the satellite dish that you were adjusting. I was an identity, a life force that all humans contain. I guess you would call it your mind or perhaps even soul. We have the ability to exit our physical bodies when we travel vast distances through space-time. Tell me, am I on Earth Alpha?"

"Earth, yes but I've never heard of the alpha being added to the name."

"And this is the late twenty-first century?"

"No, it's only the first decade of the century."

Shelley frowned. "So that's why... Oh well, it doesn't matter. I am still alive and that is a blessing."

"Okay," Rhett retorted. "You trust me but as I see it, it is you who owes me an explanation. Can I trust you? By your actions to date I see no real reason why I should." He sucked in a breath. "You're the woman running around the village in the nude and those clothes you're wearing were stolen from a local clothes line, weren't they?"

More tears formed in her eyes. "Can I?' she asked as she reached for a tissue from a nearby box.

"Help yourself," Rhett said in a softer tone. Perhaps he shouldn't be so unsympathetic. "Sit down while I make myself a coffee then I want an explanation, Shelley; a plausible one that I can comprehend. Understand?"

Shelley caught his eyes and smiled. "I'll tell you how I arrived. Afterwards you can decide if my trust in you is reciprocated. If not, I'll leave and you'll never hear from me again. Is that fair?"

"Yes," Rhett replied. "I'll get my coffee..."

"As I said," Shelley said a few moments later. "I arrived as a electronic identity through your dish. Think of me being like a ball of lightning..."

When she sat on the couch and began her tale Rhett listened with fascination and growing interest

*

Shelley had no idea how long she had been in the rescue pod after the battle cruiser's destruction. It could have been anything from a few moments to decades.

"We have reached your destination, Shelley," Grass the computer said through the pod's hidden loudspeakers. "There is a problem."

"What is it?" Shelley sat up and climbed out of the cocoon that had encased her. As usual after the deep sleep, she felt hungry and thirsty. Now awake, she needed food, water and air to maintain her body. As well, the metallic suit that she wore felt filthy.

"There are no reception stations on this planet. Due to malfunctions that our robots could not repair, my orbit can be maintained for only seventeen local days, our air supply will last ten, you have food for three days and water for six."

Shelley paled. "Are there any other pods around?"

"None." As usual, Grass offered no further explanation.

"So I am alone. What a do you suggest?"

"Your DNA profile is in my memory banks so you will be able to rebuild your physical body once you are on the surface."

"Meaning?"

"I explained the concept of being an identity before you went into your deep sleep."

"My brain waves are copied into an electronic force field. I'll be conscious and will be able to move by just thinking about what I wish to do."

"Basically, that is correct. Tell me the limits you will encounter."

At times Grass sounded like an old school teacher Shelley remembered from school. He had been a grouchy old guy but, on hindsight, had been the best teacher she'd ever had.

"I am limited by what my physical body would need, and would not survive without air for three minutes, water for a day and food for a week. Air can be carried with me in my identity form but I will need to become human again to take in water and food."

"You learned well." A compliment from the computer was rare and Shelley smiled. "I have incorporated a remote device to reactivate your body after you reach your destination. In is not a perfect answer but is all I can offer at this time."

"Why?"

"Primitive surveillance equipment on Earth Alpha below can trace this ship so I have had to change your final destination."

"Earth Alpha, the original planet where humans came from?"

Shelley gasped.

"Your branch of humanity, Shelley. You are but one of..."

"I know," Shelley interrupted. The last thing she needed now was a history lecture. "If I can't land in eastern United States where you say others from my space-time operate a portal, where can I go?"

"I will enter the atmosphere over the southern continent called Antarctica. It is a frozen barren place containing only a few research facilities. When our hull begins to burn up in the atmosphere, you will be in an identity who will need to drop down to a landing, yourself. By then, I shall cease to operate."

"But where?' Shelley gasped.

"There are two places, a continent of Australia which I would advise you avoid as they have primitive defence facilities. Off to the east is a small island nation of New Zealand. It has a high standard of human life, a small population and no defence force."

"Meaning?"

"As an identity you may be seen by local radar. Fighter aircraft, such as the Australians operate could lock onto and explode near you. It is an extremely archaic method of defending skies over a country but, unfortunately, it could still neutralise your life forces."

"Do I have any alternative choices?"

"Yes, there are always alternatives."

"So what else could I do?"

"Die," Grass replied in a passionless voice.

*

The drop was terrifying. Shelley was totally alone and flying over an ocean. After the ice of the frozen continent, it had been a welcomed sight but she had no way of knowing the passage of time except by using the sun as a reference. She became worried. What if there was no island and she had to land in the ocean? At some stage she would have to revert back to her physical body and would either drown, starve or die of thirst.

She switched her mind and tried to remember everything she had been taught. Of course she could follow an electronic signal from one of the numerous satellites down. But where to? Of course, she had to find a receiving station. She went into a trancelike state and let the identity fail-safe systems remotely operate. Again this was terrifying but it had to be done.

Shelley awoke to find herself dropping straight down over a small town; the ocean was to her left and rolling brown hills the other way. Before she could even switch to manual flight she landed on a male with his hand on a metallic saucer above a house. She hit his hand and a thousand thoughts rushed into her own mind including his language. It was English, a crude version of her own language but easy to absorb. He was male but she sensed he was a kind man recovering from some sadness. His thoughts were hers and she felt his pain as she burned his skin.

She could not stay there or her mind would enter his. She would become him. She knew this man was not the ruthless male she knew from home. But she had no wish to become a male nor could she expect him to absorb her female mind.

She seized control and flew out of his hand, narrowly avoided a nearby tree and flew towards the ocean. Now that was stupid. She turned and dropped, exhausted between some spiky grass growing out of a valley of sand dunes.

There was a hiss a bump and Shelley found herself lying on the sand. She was human again but nude and alone in a new world.

*

Shelley stared at Rhett. " Did I say something?"

Rhett frowned. "You just told me of your arrival. You were an identity... Don't you remember?"

Shelley frowned. "An identity is when our life force departs from our physical body. Is that right?"

"That's what you told me."

"I remember nothing except your name, Rhett." Shelley whispered.

"But you just told me what happened to you."

"What did I say?"

Rhett repeated what he remembered of Shelley's conversation.

"And I told you all that?"

"Yes."

"I remember nothing" She frowned. "Not a thing."

Rhett studied her. Was the story she'd told just a fantasy or was she lying now when she said she'd forgotten everything?"

"So what do you remember?" he said with caution in his voice.

"I have a vague recollection of flying over the beach and waking up with no clothes on in the early morning. I was scared and embarrassed. I remained hidden all day but eventually had to do something. I crept down to a stream and had a drink but was tired and hungry. I am as honest as you, Rhett but had to do something. That's why I stole the clothes. Unfortunately, I was seen and actually chased by some males. I was terrified again, found a culvert to hide in and wasn't found."

"And then came here?" Rhett asked.

Shelley nodded. "I know everything about you Rhett. Your memories are mine, now."

"All of them?' Rhett gasped.

"I guess. If I think back, I remember your memories but not my own." She pouted.

"Go on." Rhett encouraged.

"Lesley wasn't a loving wife who got ill with cancer and died. She was a bitch that you only stayed with out of duty and sympathy."

Rhett stared at the young alien woman. He had told nobody of those agonising last two years, not even his closest friends, Val or Jerry. He put it all down to her to the disease and treatment. But even before she had the lump in her beast diagnosed as cancerous, their marriage was just a sham. After her taunts after he had found out about an affair with a guy where she worked he was about to walk away. However, it was not to be.

Shelley reached out and took his hands. They felt so soft and … this was stupid. She was a stranger that he'd only known for less than an hour.

"Can I stay?"

"Yes," Rhett said almost too quickly. "You can sleep in Val and Jerry's room. I sleep in the hut. It's that a small bunkhouse on the back lawn."

"Can't you stay in here," Shelley replied. "I mean..."

"I guess I can sleep in the girls' room." He pointed to a door next to the kitchen. "What now? "

"I'll help you paint the deck," Shelley said.

*

CHAPTER TWO

The expression on old Matthew's face that evening when Shelley turned up on the deck in Val's shorts and top was priceless. He peered at her, muttered a brief "Hello" and raised his eyebrows at Rhett. Otherwise he was very discrete.

Shelley greeted him like an old friend and began painting. When she chatted away, Rhett couldn't stop himself gasping. Everything she talked about was from his memory. The workplace was his, chatter about small home incidences were from his life and even general affairs about local news and government happenings were items that he took an interest in. She even repeated his opinions about things.

"My best friend, Janice is getting married in a couple on months," Shelley rattled on. She bent over to paint the wooden steps and displayed a cleavage that Rhett couldn't fail to notice. "Nice girl but a bit promiscuous."

Her eyes caught Rhett's and he flushed bright red but for a different reason than the view of her breasts. Janice worked at the office with him and they had had a clandestine affair just before Lesley's death. She stopped the affair and, almost immediately afterwards became engaged to another guy. He'd found out later that she had been seeing him all the time. Her callousness affected him almost as much as Lesley's death.

With three of them working, the deck was completed in a little over an hour. Shelley stood up with perspiration showing damp spots under her armpits and her face was now sunburnt. She grinned, placed her brush in a container and turned to Matthew.

"Beer?" she asked. "Rhett always has a cold beer after a hot hour's work." She turned to Rhett. "Don't you, Dear?"

"Of course," Rhett muttered and watched as she stepped down onto the lawn and walked around the side of the house to the other entrance at the back.

"Like the girlfriend," Matthew said. "If I was a couple of decades younger..." He stared out unblinking from shaggy eyebrows. "You know that story I told you earlier?"

"Yes..." Now what was coming?

"The clothes turned up, all washed, folded and placed in a plastic bag. Pauline Smith found them hanging from her clothesline. Strange, isn't it?"

So that was why the spin drier was on earlier and Shelley had later disappeared for quarter an hour. "A teenage prank I'd say. Kid stole them, her mum found out and told her to take them back, " Rhett muttered.

The old man rubbed his chin. "Yeah, could be that."

Shelley returned and the conversation ceased. However, a few moments later, another strange happening jerked any complacency from Rhett.

"I've never seen anything like it," Matthew muttered and stared out across the section.

A whirlwind of dust and litter blew in across the road and sort of bounced off the front bushes. Clouds of dry leaves, dirt and lawn clippings swirled everywhere as it swirled towards them. A flock of gulls flew out of the way, squawking while the neighbour's cat ran across their lawn with its tail fluffed up in fright.

"Get down!" Rhett screamed and instinctively grabbed Shelley to protect her.

With a bang a pile of dirt exploded up in the garden a few metres away. Dirt spun in the air, dropped back and left a hole the size of an inverted road works cone. Afterwards the whirlwind dissipated as quickly as it arrived.

"I'm okay but thank you," Shelley squeezed Rhett's hand and caught his eyes. Her expression appeared to warn him to be cautious.

So the whirlwind wasn't a coincidence! She had something to do with it. After all the other events, this was not really surprising.

*

"Come and look." Shelley said half an hour later after Matthew had finally left. She walked across the lawn and reached into the newly formed hole.

Rhett paled as he watched for the girl's hand disappear... literally! He could see her arm and wrist but nothing else. It was as if a saw had cut it off. There was just a blurry stump where her wrist should have been. An instant later, her hand and fingers appeared reappeared holding a metal sphere the size of a child's beach ball.

"It was hidden by a light refraction shield," she said with a far away look in her eyes. "It was sent by Grass, the computer. I guess he couldn't create a direct portal."

"Portal?' Rhett gasped.

Shelley still appeared to be looking through Rhett rather than at him. "I arrived eighty years too far back in time. Humans on Earth Alpha hadn't even met the girifa or other extraterrestrial life forms at that time."

"This time, Shelley. We're here, now."

"Of course. Sorry."

She handed the ball to him and just stood motionless when he glowered. Though he had anticipated that the ball would have weigh several kilograms but it was almost weightless.

"Your light refraction shield?" he asked as he handed it back.

Shelley jerked and her eyes focused on his. "My what? "

Rhett gulped. Had she forgotten what she had just said again? "What did you just tell me?" he asked.

Shelley appeared frightened. "I know I was talking to you about this emergency survival kit that followed me here." She glanced at the object in her hand and sucked on her bottom lip. "Why did that girl, Janice mate with you and reject you when you were so lonely and vulnerable?" she suddenly blurted out.

"That's life," Rhett shrugged. "I thought we might have made a go of it."

"I'd never do that," Shelley's eyes met his and again she looked empathetic. Her expression changed to a smile. "Anyway, let's see what's in the emergency survival kit that followed me down."

*

"Damn," Shelley said a few moments later and placed the sphere back on the kitchen table. "It knows who I am but will not open."

"And it told you that?' Rhett replied.

"I think so."

She held it out and he saw a series of waving lines curling over the surface from the equator, through both hemispheres before they disappeared into the poles. The lines were a light blue that faded to white at the top and bottom. When Shelley placed the sphere on the bench and let it go, the lines disappeared.

"Now you pick it up."

Rhett did. It felt slightly warm but the sphere just remained solid looking.

"That's strange," the girl muttered.

"What?"

"The colours. It rejected you and only partially accepted me."

"Meaning?"

Shelley shrugged. "Perhaps I am too tense. My blood pressure could be up."

"So what do we do?"

"Come back tomorrow when, hopefully I'm more relaxed."

"You'd think it was alive, reading your emotions like that."

"No, it is just a machine, Rhett. At least it is not one that can take over our minds and control us." She stopped and flushed.

"You've forgotten everything you just said again, haven't you?"

Shelley smiled. "No, I know what I said. I just don't know how I knew the information I talked about."

Rhett grinned. "Well that's an improvement. It seems that nothing will happen now so let me show you our beach. There's still an hour of daylight left and it's a beautiful evening."

*

With so many families gone, Riversdale Beach was relatively quiet. The surf patrol was still on duty with red and yellow flags marking the safe swimming area that evening. Twenty to thirty people swam in the surf, couples walked along the sand, three campfires smoked away and several children and the not so young built sandcastles before the tide.

For several moments Rhett and Shelley walked in silence before she went over to the surf. She jumped a line of foam and just stood there smiling as the next wave crashed before her and water swirled around her toes.

"Do you like the ocean?" Rhett asked.

"It is beautiful, so peaceful that the birds are even happy." She pointed to a line of seagulls who hardly moved as they walked by. Can we go for a swim?"

"Can you?"

"Swim? I think I can for I feel quite confident." She glanced at some teenagers nearby. "I don't know why I was worried about being seen. Why do they even bother?" She nodded at two teenage girls in bikinis.

"I think Val left some togs at home. They're more modest than that girl's."

"Togs?" Shelley giggled. "Of course, they're the swimming suits. Some of your words are still strange. Languages change, don't they?"

"Even in our world," Rhett said. "Millions of people speak English yet some words are only used by our little country. We call those things on your feet jandals but in other places they're thongs or flip-flops."

"But why?"

"Just customs I guess."

They headed back home and checked the sphere that lay lifeless on the sink but nothing was different. They changed, grabbed towels and minutes later were diving through waves. Shelley was capable and was soon body surfing in with the crashing breakers. They laughed and played, splashed each other and ran into the surf together. Finally they walked up to their towels and dried themselves.

"You need to be careful," Rhett said.

"Why?"

"Lucky it is late in the day but you're still sunburnt. You'll be sore tomorrow."

"Will I?"

Rhett grinned. "I'm sure you won't be too bad."

"But pale bodies are ugly?"

"No," Rhett whispered. "Anything but."

*

Morning arrived and Rhett's first recollection was the smell of bacon frying. He opened his eyes, sat up and banged his head on the bunk above. Of course, he was in the kids' room and had slept on a lower bunk. After rubbing his head he dressed and walked into the kitchen. Shelley had already had a shower for her hair was wet. She smiled at him.

"You look a mess," she said. "Go and shower. Breakfast will be ready soon."

After breakfast, Shelley looked up at him and he saw something was wrong. Her face had drained into a ghastly white and perspiration formed on her brow and neck. Within seconds her top was damp and her hands shook.

"I don't feel too good," she muttered, went to stand but collapsed sideways. Her chair fell over and she hit the floor with a thud.

"Shelley!" Rhett screamed.

He was beside her within a second, bent down and touched her forehead. She was now feverish and moaning. Her whole body jerked and foam edged out the side of her clenched teeth.

"Shelley!" He picked up her shaking body and headed for the couch. She was heavy but just before he laid her down her weight disappeared. "No!" he screamed for the girl in his arms became transparent; he could see right through her!

She vanished. A yellow pulsing tennis ball under a bundle of clothes was in his hands. It vibrated and enlarged, he staggered under the sudden weight in his arms and blinked. Shelley reappeared beneath the clothes, still unconscious but looking slightly better.

"I'll get you to the doctor," Rhett cried. "Hang in there. I'll get help!"

*

There was no local doctor but the fifty-kilometre journey to Masterton through a windy road was completed in forty minutes. Just before Rhett turned his Toyota in through the local hospital Accident and Emergency entrance, Shelley sighed and her eyes opened.

"Rhett!" she whispered. "Where are we?"

"We're at the hospital. It won't be long now."

They parked and Shelley insisted on walking into the waiting room. It was relatively quiet and the wait wasn't too long.

"I'll be fine," she said after a nurse indicated she should follow her into a curtained off cubical.

A half an hour dragged by before Shelley reappeared with a sheepish expression on her face. Rhett stood and took her hands. "What was it?"

"A nasty strain of flu. Apparently, my body had no immunity. I told the doctor I'd just flown in from England. She said I could have picked it up in the Hong Kong stopover." She bit on her lip and stared at the ground.

"That's not the full story is it, Shelley?"

She nodded but couldn't look directly at him.

"Shelley!"

She looked up. "There was something. The doctor wishes to speak to my next of kin, whatever that means. I said you were. Is that okay?"

"Yes. I'll see what she wants."

*

The doctor, a woman in her early forties, extended her hand when Rhett walked in the cubical. "Mrs Shelley Pennant's husband?"

Rhett almost replied that Shelley wasn't his wife but hesitated. It wasn't important at the moment. "Yes."

He never caught her name but listened, fascinated to the information the doctor divulged.

"When I was examining your wife her heart stopped."

"What! ... But she's fine and actually looks better."

"That's it," the doctor replied. "For ten seconds, I guess it was she had no pulse what-so-ever. I was about to call a crash team to try to restart her heart when it started on its own." She frowned. "Does your wife have a history of any heart condition?"

"Not since I've known her."

"That's what she told me but she appeared ill at ease, shall we say?"

"Shelley does become self conscious at times."

"I would advise you to seek help with your local GP and get a referral to a specialist." She glanced at her notes. "I could do it but Mrs Pennant said your doctor in Wellington had been your physician for years."

Rhett coughed. Shelley had used his memory again. "He is, but I am more concerned about the immediate situation. We're at present staying in Riversdale, which is quite a way from emergency treatment. Will her heart suddenly stop again?"

"It is unlikely. I think the problem was brought about by her extremely high temperature, over forty degrees, and the virus." The doctor frowned. "That is unusual, too. After her heart started her pulse was normal, as was her blood pressure and temperature. All symptoms of the virus had also vanished. It was as if her body had recharged itself."

"She's a determined woman," Rhett replied. He thanked the doctor and returned to Shelley.

*

As they drove back, Shelley just stared out the window at the brown hills, the houses, animals along the way but said little. She turned and sucked on her bottom lip. "You are annoyed with me, aren't you?"

"No. Why should I be?"

"I used your name and memories to give that doctor information. I shouldn't have lied."

"Why not?' Rhett laughed. "It was a logical thing to do and I'm quite honoured."

"Pretending to be your wife?"

Rhett nodded. "And your heart? Do you know what happened?"

'Of course," Shelley replied. "I couldn't tell the doctor, though."

"But you'll tell me."

"I became an identity and left my body. The doctor was so concerned about my condition that she never noticed me hovering by the ceiling behind her. As soon as I realised what had happened I returned to my physical self."

"Oh my God but why did you do it in the first place?"

"I didn't. It just happened. I had no control but think a fail-safe system was activated by my condition."

"You did it earlier, too," Rhett replied and told her of his experience when he lifted her to the couch. "Can you remember that?"

"No but by your explanation, they were slightly different. At least my body didn't disappear before the doctor." She grinned. "Now that would have taken some explaining, wouldn't it?"

"And you know why?"

"Not really. I think my sub-conscious realised it would have been dangerous to disappear so it left my body behind." She thought for a moment. "No, it was more likely that I had to be out of it so repairs could be carried out. When I awoke, I felt fine and now have no symptoms of the flu at all. My own immune system has controlled it."

"So I never needed to take you to the hospital in the first place?"

Shelley laughed. "Probably not but I'm glad you did. It proves what a kind man you are." She walked up and kissed him on the cheek. "Thank you. It's nice to know you care."

*

When they returned to Rhett's place, the sphere still sat on the sink and Shelley reached for it. Immediately, it became warm and the lines spiralled out. They appeared brighter this time.

"My temperature is normal," she said. "Oh Rhett..." She stared at him. "I can't let it go!"

The ball pulsed and grew into a ball of white that surrounded her. Without hesitation, Rhett reached forward and grabbed her waist. A high-pitched screaming sound filled his ears and the light became so bright he had to shut his eyes. Shelley was being pulled away from him...

She screamed and he pulled her in close with a bear hug. The light dimmed so he opened his eyes. Shelley was still in his arms and staring, terrified beyond him. She reached under his arm and grabbed something!

"A portal has opened," she screamed. "Don't let me go!"

She was hanging onto the edge of an ancient looking oaken door. He could see the stained wood; the panels it was made from and a rusty old-fashioned latch on the right side.

The light returned to normal. The door, inside an equally old dark frame, sat in front of the table. There were no walls, just the door and frame. It was ajar and Shelley and himself were wedged in the gap between the door and this frame.

But they were being sucked in. He dared not let her go so just clung to her. Shelley now used both hands to try to hold the doorframe but the force was too great! Her fingers must have lost their grip for they suddenly pitched forward, through the door into bright sunlight,

They crashed onto gravel with Rhett still clinging to her. He heard the door bang shut and the force pulling them forward stopped. He stared out.

Way below was a forest of deciduous trees, not New Zealand native bush, but more like the forests of central Europe he had once visited on an overseas trip. He turned and almost lost his grip on Shelley when he saw their predicament.

They were on the edge of a gigantic cliff that dropped sheer and vertical down to the forest several hundred metres below. He cautiously lifted his head and turned. The door was behind them but it was now embedded in a wall, an ancient stone wall that was along one side of half a room.

Half a room! It took his racing mind a few seconds to make sense of what his eyes saw. It appeared that they were in an ancient room of a building that had been in an earthquake or more likely a landslide. The front of the room had slipped away down the cliff and the door was now teetering on the edge of an abyss with only a metre of stone floor left before empty space.

"Are you okay?" he asked Shelley.

"Yes," she whispered. "The kitchen!'

Rhett looked up. He had distinctly heard the door bang shut but now it was slightly ajar. Through the gap he could see the sink, cupboards and refrigerator. They were though the door but looking back at his Riversdale house.

*

CHAPTER THREE

"Rhett!" Shelley whispered and wriggled out from under him. "The other door!"

He frowned and looked in the direction where his companion was focused. There was another door along the wall, one that looked less substantial than the one they'd just been pulled through. It was more like an interior door rather than an external one. His heart leaped for the old brass handle was turning.

Before either of them could comment further, the door opened. Behind, everything appeared dark but as it moved further out he saw a hand holding the inside knob. A girl of about twelve stood there!

She appeared scared with wide brown eyes that stared at them. Except for being crumpled and dirty, her jacket, top and black jeans would not have been noticed in any modern city street Her face itself was filthy with lines down the cheeks as if she'd been crying and matted blonde hair hung over her face. Her hands appeared scratched with dirty broken fingernails. She wore a pair of old leather boots on her feet.

When the girl spoke, Rhett could only decipher an occasional word. It was a high-pitched abbreviated English spoken at high velocity and jumbled with alien sounds.

"Listen!" Shelley gasped and grabbed his hand. A minor shock jolted him and the stranger's words reassembled in his mind.

"Are you my parents?" she asked. "Rhett and Shelley Pennant?"

Oh hell, what was this all about? She got Shelley's name muddled up with his but actually knew them.

"Don't you remember me? I'm Dee?" The youngster sucked on her bottom lip nervously, just as Shelley had done a couple of times since he'd met her.

Rhett flushed for a vision entered his mind, one of a little girl about three holding his hand. They were standing with Shelley beside a bed where a woman held a newly born baby in her arms. She smiled at them and held the baby out. He reached for it and the vision faded.

Shelley glanced at him but appeared as flabbergasted as he felt. She gave his hand a slight squeeze and turned to the girl

"Dee," she said with caution in her voice. "What are you doing here?"

"Trying to find you." The girl's words turned to sobs. "Oh Mum, you need to help get Corwin before they do."

Corwin... that was the baby's name! Rhett didn't know how he knew but he was certain it was true.

"Future memories," Shelley whispered. "You remember something that has yet to take place." She turned to Dee. "Where is

Corwin, Sweetheart?"

"Down in the valley. He's caught in a cage. When the girifa come, they'll kill him. They only keep girls like myself and kill the boys."

"Why?" Rhett gasped.

"Breeding," Shelley whispered. "Female humans are kept for breeding. Only a few males are needed so most are killed. I'll tell you more about it later. We need to get Dee home."

"Home!"

"The portal!" Shelley nodded at the oak door they'd come through.

"But her brother?"

"Mum!" Dee interrupted. "Please help!"

"We will," Shelley stepped forward and cuddled the girl. Dee just clung on and burst into uncontrolled sobs.

"But if we go back, won't we be cut off?" Rhett asked.

"I don't know." Again she turned to Dee. "Don't look down. Reach out for Daddy's hand, he'll take you though the portal and home to our world."

"But what about Corwin?" the girl sobbed. "I can't leave him."

"You know about time-space quantum physics, don't you?"

"A little."

"So you know that the time you're in our world won't make any difference here? When we come back it will be exactly the time as it is now."

Dee nodded. "You'll come back?"

"Of course, Dee," Rhett whispered. He reached out, grabbed the warm hand and watched as she stepped in beside him. He edged along the wall, back to the portal and pushed the door open.

There was no suction but just a minor feeling of disorientation as he guided her through. A moment later, Shelley followed and they were back in their Riversdale kitchen.

"Mum, Daddy where are we?" Dee gasped.

"Earth Alpha, Daddy's world, Dee."

"It's not just a dream world?"

"No it exists and we're in it."

Dee relaxed a little as she gazed around. Her eyes settled on a bowl of fruit. "I'm hungry, Mum. Can I have a banana?"

"Anything Sweetheart,"

Dee smiled. "You always called me that, Mum," she whispered.

"Called you what?"

"Sweetheart and Daddy called me His Little Heart-throb."

Oh hell! Rhett remembered saying the words as he bounced a tiny girl on his knees.

" I know it sounds silly but what was the date when you found us?" Shelley asked.

"Tuesday. 24th of August I think."

"The year, Dee."

Shelley gasped at Dee's reply.

"What is it?" Rhett whispered but Shelley brought a finger to her lips.

A few moments later when Dee was in the shower Shelley came back and explained.

"I remember the date of my arrival in my time. If Dee comes from my world as I suspect she does, it is fourteen years after I left," she said. "We could quite easily be her parents."

Rhett flushed at the implication of Shelley's words. "But we've never..."

"Not yet," she interrupted. "But unless we want to destroy Dee so she never existed, sometime in the future you'll father a child within me." She reached out for his hands. "I never planned this, Rhett. You could call it fate, I guess."

"I don't mind," he replied.

Without thinking he reached forward and kissed her lightly on the lips. She kissed him back and held on close for a moment before she stepped back, squeezed his hand and headed back to the bathroom.

*

A few moments later, the three sat on the deck in the sunshine with Dee dressed in Ava's clothes while the ones she had arrived in were being washed. Though a little tight, the clothes were quite adequate. Shelley had tended to her wounds and was now combing her hair out.

"You came though to those ruins where you found us alone?" Rhett asked as he placed a Band-Aid over a deep scratch on Dee's arm.

She nodded.

"Weren't you scared?"

Dee gazed up at him and nodded again.

"But how did you know where to come, Sweetheart?" Shelley asked.

"Didn't you notice, Mum?" Dee replied.

"Notice what?"

Dee put a hand up to an ear. "My earrings are the same as yours."

"What!" Shelley examined the almost insignificant pearl earrings that Dee wore. She gasped and glanced up at Rhett.

"She's right. They a family heirloom passed on though our family and are a duplicate set of the ones I'm wearing." She pulled her hair aside and Rhett noticed a similar set in her earlobes. "The tradition was that we always wore a pair. I think there were three sets."

"Yes. They're more than just rings, Mum. Didn't you ever use them?"

"Use them? For what, Dee?"

"That's how I knew where to come. The direction finder in them led me to your portal. If I went the wrong way, the rings would beep or go silent. As long as I followed the humming they made, I knew I was going the right way. When the beep became a steady hum, I knew I was close to you."

"Do you remember who these girifa are?" Rhett asked.

Shelley screwed her nose up. "It seems that my memory returns if I need the information is helpful to me. There are many intelligent species in the known universe," Shelley replied. "The main two are humans like ourselves and the girifa whose ancient ancestors were reptiles, not mammals. They are cold blooded and the females lay eggs rather than give birth to offspring. In most settled planets they live peacefully with humans but on some worlds they are our enemies."

"And your world?"

"In my time we tolerated each other by remaining separated. However, wars were often raged between us. The worse girifa used captured humans as a food supply in the same way that we farm animals for beef, pork or mutton."

"Oh hell," Rhett stuttered. "And that's what's happening in your world, Dee?"

"I think so," the girl whispered. "We had nothing to do with the girifa until the raids started. They'd attack our villages and kill the males and older women. The other ladies and the girls were taken away. We never found out where."

"And your village was attacked?" Shelley asked.

Dee nodded. "Some elders helped us escape. However the girifa followed us. Corwin and I hid in the forest but he got caught in this cage. That was when my earring began to beep. One of the village elders told me that if I was ever in danger this would happen. If it did, I needed to turn until the beeps were close together they became a hum and I'd find my parents." She glanced up. "It worked, didn't it?"

"Yes, Sweetheart," Shelley said, "It did."

*

While Shelley and Dee packed a backpack with food, Rhett filled a larger one with everything that he thought would be helpful on the other side of the portal. This included warm clothes as Dee said it was cooler there, cutting tools and an assortment of gear he often used when tramping. He stood thinking before he added a coil of rope, and, almost as an afterthought, a carbon dioxide fire extinguisher that was clamped to a fitting near the veranda.

Though she said nothing, Dee was becoming more anxious. She tried to hide her feelings but wasn't interested in Rhett's suggestion of visiting the beach.

"Come on," Shelley whispered. "We'll achieve nothing by staying longer. Dee is frantic to get back and help her brother."

"So we'll go." Rhett pulled the curtains and locked the doors. "Just in case someone comes and sees the old door sitting in the middle of the room."

Shelley followed by Dee and finally himself, walked though the portal to the somewhat scary ledge. On close inspection, though, the path above the cliff appeared stable and, as long as they kept to the wall, was not dangerous. It reminded Rhett of the time as a teenager he'd walked across the maintenance walkway slung below a railway viaduct. As long as he didn't look down it was quite safe.

They walked though the second door and into new territory. It was a musty stone corridor, water stained, covered in grim, dust and cobwebs. The only sign of anyone being there were Dee's footprints across a muddy section.

"What is this place?" he asked.

"An ancient monastery. At school they told us it was built a thousand years ago by monks who believed that they were closer to heaven at the top of a mountain."

They lapsed in silence and followed Dee down a circular stairwell and through another corridor to an entrance. Here, the front door had long gone and vegetation grew through the crumpled remains of what would have once been a courtyard and an exit outside where an overgrown stone track led through grass and boulders. After five minutes walking in a downwards spiral, the building they had come from appeared above them to their left. The two white towers in sight hid the crumbling back where they had arrived. Slits served as windows except for a large bay window at the top of one tower. The whole structure sat above a bank of white clouds with dense forest further below. In a less stressful situation it would have been a delightful view. Underfoot, the steps were worn and slippery in shady sections. The handrail had long gone and now consisted of a few stone posts with rotting rails protruding.

"And you climbed all the way up here by yourself?" Shelley gasped.

"Yes."

"Oh Sweetheart, I am so proud of you."

Dee glanced up and smiled slightly. "My earrings told me to keep going, I had to help Corwin and there was nobody else."

"What about the elders who helped you escape?" Rhett asked.

Dee shrugged. "They never came back. I think they were caught."

"And how long did it take to reach the monastery?" Rhett pressed.

"Forever," Dee admitted. "I never knew it would be so far. I stopped several times and wondered if I should go back to Corwin. Once, I even walked back a few metres but my earrings got angry so I kept going up."

"By beeping, Sweetheart?" Shelley asked.

"Yes. If I pretended there was a little man in my ears, it wasn't so hard being by myself. I really knew it was just a tracking device but the thought made me feel better."

Shelley slipped back a step, placed an arm around Dee's shoulders and hugged her tightly. She reached back with her other hand. Rhett took it and squeezed.

"We're family, Dee and whatever happens you'll never be alone again," she whispered. "And that's a promise."

Dee never replied but tears slid down her cheeks as she stepped down yet another stone step.

*

Without warning, screams and crying drifted through the trees in the trackless forest.

"It's Corwin," Dee whimpered.

The distressed girl broke into a run but Shelley was faster. She grabbed Dee and held the crying, kicking girl in a firm grip. "Stop it!" she whispered. "It won't help."

But Dee continued to fight.

Shelley was too strong, though and managed to pin her arms in with a tight hold. "Do something!" she howled at Rhett.

"Hold Dee here!" he gasped as he tore forward. He reached back and by the time he was through the trees ahead he had dropped his backpack but had his only weapon in his hand, the fire extinguisher.

A bell shaped wire cage was suspended by a rope below an oak tree branch and a metre above the ground. But Rhett's eyes were on the two men standing on each side of the cage with short spears in their hands. They were the strangest men he'd ever seen. Both were almost two metres tall, slim and dressed in military fatigues with solid boots. Their heads were bald and hairless, completely, with not even a sign of eyebrows or facial hair. They had human like facial features but no ears at all.

The men were so intent on using their spears to poke a terrified little boy cringing inside a cage that they never noticed Rhett.

"Bastards!" Rhett screeched and ran forward.

He raised the fire extinguisher and squeezed the trigger. A cloud of white carbon dioxide hissed from the hose and bathed the creatures in a white cloud. They swung around and Rhett saw one stare at him with terror in its eyes. It staggered and dropped to the ground. The second creature flung an arm out but its legs crumpled. It also collapsed onto the ground.

Rhett was ready for them to recover and attack... but they didn't. Both creatures lay in two heaps on the ground, lifeless without even an sign of breathing.

Horrified, Rhett stood back. He looked a up, straight into the eyes of the little boy. A flash of relief replaced the terror in the boy's expression. His lips quivered as he glanced at the comatose bodies before he lifted his eyes and cried out.

"Dee!" he howled.

Dee, followed closely by Shelley, ran into view with her arms extended and hair flying out behind. "What have they done to you, Corwin?" she screamed.

Shelley arrived, hugged Dee from behind and stood looking at the bodies.

"Reptilians," she whispered.

"There was nothing else I can do." Rhett muttered. "I didn't expect to kill them."

"You didn't," Shelley replied. "They're in suspended animation. They're cold blooded and can't remain conscious in cold temperatures. It's already quite cool in the forest here and they'd have been quite lethargic anyway. That cloud of freezing stuff from your fire extinguisher did the rest. They'll awaken in an hour or so, faster if the sunlight reaches them."

"They never looked lethargic when I arrived," Rhett muttered.

"Get Corwin down!" Dee screamed. "He's hurt."

"Only a little," the boy replied. He nursed a bloodstained arm and smiled. "You got help like you said you would. I thought you'd never come." His eyes watered and he burst into quiet sobs.

It took only a moment to cut the rope and lower the cage to the forest floor but longer to cut Corwin free. While Both Shelley and Dee comforted the little boy and handed him food to eat, Rhett tipped the cage sideways and used his wire cutters to slice through the fifteen or more joins that linked to the circular base.

"It dropped on him from above," Dee explained. "When he struggled to get out he tripped over a rope. It pulled him up under the tree and the bottom sprung shut. I couldn't open it or cut the thing down." She glanced at her brother. "I'm sorry, Corwin," she whispered.

"But you're here. That's all that matters." Corwin wiped away tears from his eyes as he sat with his knees up on the tipped over cage. "Who are these people?"

"Your mummy and daddy," Dee whispered. "I found them."

"Almost got it," Rhett murmured. He cut through the last three strands while Shelley pulled back the bars. These were hinged to the outside and moved easily.

When the bottom bars were opened out, she reached in and slid the little boy onto the grass. He glanced at her, muttered a thanks and turned, sobbing to his sister.

It took a few moments to pacify him and get the full story. Corwin only added a little information. After Dee had left he'd spent a terrified night alone, sleeping spasmodically and awoke stiff and hungry to find it was morning.

"But I never went through a night," Dee gasped.

"Perhaps you missed it when you came through the portal,"

Shelley said.

"A group of reppies arrived and..."

"There were others?" Rhett asked

Corwin nodded.

"Do you know where they are?"

"Most of them went off. It was only after they left that the two men began teasing and poking me."

"We'd better head back, then," Rhett whispered. "I don't like the idea of more of these creatures being around. Will you be able to walk, Corwin?'

"Yes," Corwin whispered. "I'm okay now. Really I am."

"And so brave," Shelley replied. She hugged him and placed a kiss on his cheek. "Come on. If you get tired Daddy will give you a ride on his back."

Corwin flushed but after looking at Dee for approval, smiled and took another bite from the apple he was munching.

*

CHAPTER FOUR

Rhett followed the indiscreet marks he had made on various objects in this trackless section under the oak trees. He'd placed a stone on a tree root, pulled up a piece of grass or snapped off a twig every few metres along the way. Years before he had belonged to an orienteering club at high school and, until now, had never used the skills he had learned.

After ten minutes Dee caught up to him and tugged on his sleeve.

Rhett glanced down. "Is there something wrong?" he asked.

"We're being followed," she whispered. "Listen!"

He stopped and waved at the others to listen. However, he heard nothing in the silent forest. There wasn't even wind in the trees. A far off bird called out and he thought he could hear a faint sound of gurgling water off to the left but that was it.

"What did you hear, Dee?" He too kept his voice to a whisper.

"Footsteps but they've stopped. When we did, so did they?"

"What way?"

Dee nodded to their left and indicated with her eyes that the sound came from further back.

Shelley came up. "I thought I heard something, too," she whispered. "Test it."

"How?"

"Keep walking and talk in an ordinary voice. On my signal, stop dead still and listen."

"Okay." Rhett grabbed Dee's hand, noticed that Shelley had Corwin's, and started a conversation. "I'm sure there's a duck quacking," he said. "Probably it flew over to the stream we can hear..."

After a tense couple of minutes he held his hand up, they stopped and waited. Off to their left, grass rustled and a twig snapped before everything became silent. Dee was right. Someone was there!

He reached for their only weapon, the fire extinguisher, indicated that Shelley should take Dee's hand and took up a position at the rear. He glanced around but could only see tree trunks and low branches; the ground cover consisted of short grass and dead leaves from the season before. Their own feet would have crunched on these leaves as they walked. Even if they continued in silence, any expert tracker could follow them.

"Stay here!" he hissed.

He swallowed, tensed his muscles, gave a bloodcurdling scream and charged off to the left,

It worked!

He had only charged through four trees when he saw three girifa stare up in horror from behind a massive trunk. They were dressed in military garb and it was impossible to tell their sex, not that it mattered. Rhett lifted the fire extinguisher and squeezed the trigger. A cloud of carbon dioxide hissed around the aliens.

There was coughing and spluttering and a sharp report. Rhett ducked and actually heard a whistle like a bee by his ear. One of the creatures had fired a weapon. He moved left and retreated. He was back beside the other three within seconds, grabbed the children and dived to the right behind another massive oak tree trunk.

Shelley followed!

They all crouched and Shelley hugged the children close while he lay down and wriggled forward to view the area they'd just vacated.

The three girifa appeared. One was still coughing and appeared to stagger a little but the other two were on high alert. The foremost reptilian carried a tiny weapon in its hand.

The trio stopped and stared around.

"You're wrong," said the second, a female who spoke perfect English. "They went the other way."

"That cloud gun shot came from this direction." The leader, a male, sounded angry.

"And he went straight back to the others? No, humans are highly protective of their offspring. He wanted us to come this way, which is away from the female with the children. By now he'd have circled around and back to her."

"You give these humans credit for high intelligence, Larcy," the male grumbled. "The species on this planet are little more than farm insects."

"But these were not locals." The third reptilian, also a female spoke for the first time. "It is not a hunting spear that it fired but a sophisticated cold gas that incapacitates our kind without hurting their own species."

The male glowered. "So what do you suggest, Varwil?"

"Go back and tell the others the child managed to escape from the trap. There are other cages around. We'll catch them later, anyway. There is no food in the forest and they will have to come out at some time. Once they try to return to their village one of our patrols will capture them," Varwil appeared to outrank the male.

"And if they are outworlders with the ability to materialise through space-time?"

Varwil laughed. "You're dreaming, Plue. That child we caught may be more intelligent than the natives but it was not from the future. It was more likely to come from a human province in the north. I've heard they've rebuilt quite sophisticated cities there..."

The conversation continued but Rhett couldn't make out the words after the girifa turned and retreated back through the trees. He waited until he was sure they had gone before he returned to the others.

"There's a new problem," Shelley said after Rhett related what he had overheard.

"And that is?"

"Dee has picked up a new signal in her ear and thinks we should go off to the right. That's away from the trail we left."

Rhett frowned but noticed the worried almost scared expression on the girl's face. He forced himself to remain calm and turned to her.

"It's a new sound, Dee?" he asked.

"Yes. The signal is different, sort of more high pitched."

"And it still tells you if you're going in the right direction or off course?"

"Yes. The way we're going is wrong."

"But it will take us back to the old monastery."

"I know," Dee stuttered. "But my earring has never been wrong before. What if those repees see us going up the old steps, anyway? We're completely exposed there."

"Dee's right, I think..." Shelley stopped mid-sentence, clapped a hand over her left ear and stared at Dee in amazement. "Is the sound in your ear a little like a chirping bird, Dee?"

"Yes. That's the, you're going the wrong way noise. Turn around until the sound is like a steady hum."

Shelley did and her jaw dropped. "I hear it, Rhett," she gasped. "It's very faint but I definitely hear a constant hum when I face the direction Dee says we should go."

"Dee knows," Corwin cut in. "She's never wrong. It's the place we were heading for when I got caught in the trap."

"But she came to us in the monastery," Rhett pointed out.

"I know but everything has changed," Dee said. "This is a brand new sound. I would remember the others."

"And you trust it?" Shelley whispered.

"But if you're both wrong?" Rhett argued.

"Mark our trail. If nothing happens we can come back and continue back the way we came in," Shelley suggested.

Rhett studied the three. Dee appeared quite confident now, Shelley a little more apprehensive and Corwin still nervous. However, his little lips were tight as if he was determined to back his sister up. "Half an hour. If nothing changes in that time we'll come back here. I don't want to be in this forest when it gets dark."

Shelley squeezed his hand. "Thank you," she said and turned to the children. "We'll need to go very quietly as we walk. There may be other repees around."

This time, Corwin gripped his hand while Dee held Shelley's and led them off to the right through the featureless forest. Rhett marked the trail and smiled at Corwin who began to make his own discreet markings as they moved ahead.

*

Fifteen minutes later Rhett stopped the others and guided them in behind one of the oak trunks. He indicated that they should crouch down while he crept around to look behind it.

'What is it?" Shelley whispered.

"We're being too clever," Rhett replied. "Several people are following us and I wouldn't mind betting that they're following our markers. Look!"

A shadowy figure appeared in the distance, stopped and disappeared again. Another arrived and peered ahead. Both were girifa dressed in the same military fatigues as the first they had encountered. The third alien that appeared made Rhett shudder. He was holding a sniffing lizard on a lead.

So that was how they could follow them.

"They've stopped," Shelley said. "Why don't they just come ahead and get us."

"They don't want us," Corwin said. "They want to find the magic door you came through."

Rhett frowned. "Is that just a guess, Corwin?"

The little boy shook his head. "No. I heard them talking about it when I was in the cage. That's why they didn't stop Dee when she left me to find you."

"Why didn't you tell us before?"

Corwin glanced at the ground. "I didn't think..."

"But they never followed me into the monastery," Dee said. "I would have seen them."

Corwin shrugged. "I don't know," he muttered.

Rhett noticed that Corwin was correct on one count. The aliens had definitely stopped. The dog-like lizard had been ordered to sit but it looked keen to continue. It faced their direction and glanced up at its master.

"We have to move," he said. "Dee, if we go away from your signal path, can you get us back again afterwards?"

"Yes."

"And if we leave no trail, you can still do it?"

"It got me to the monastery where I found you. I'd never even seen the mountain until I left the forest."

"Good. Hold onto my belt and don't let go, Dee. You hold Corwin's hand and Shelley, you come up the rear. Okay?"

He glanced at Shelley who nodded before heading back to a tree behind. He circled it, moved left to another tree, zigzagged by several smaller trees and continued on in a seemly haphazard manner. But he had a plan. Gradually, the object of his attention was closer. The sound of running water became louder. They were close to the stream he had heard in the distance earlier.

He moved left and circled back to a large tree they'd just left and stopped. Yes, in the distance was the sound of hushed footsteps. In spite of this tactics, the enemy stayed just out of sight behind them. The stream could help.

A moment later they came to a gap in the trees and saw the stream.

"Oh Rhett," Shelley cried.

Marshy grass grew on each side of it and the ground beneath them oozed mud. Even if they reached the stream and waded along it, the trail of footprints and crushed grass they left could easily be followed. Also, the stream was really a river and much larger than he had anticipated with green water moving sluggishly beyond the reeds. There was no way of telling how deep it was but Rhett guessed it would be far too deep to wade through. On further inspection, he found out that the river curved back like the letter U so they were surrounded on three sides by water.

He cursed. Rather than helping he had led them all into a trap that was probably exactly the intention of their pursuers

"You did it Dad," Dee whispered with joy in her voice.

Dee wasn't looking at the river but over his shoulder. Rhett turned. They were standing in front of yet another gigantic oak tree. This one had large roots that fanned out on each side of a double trunk that meet at the top of a two metre high triangle before continuing higher with branches extending out. Between the triangular sections the wood appeared artificial as if it had been smoothed by a carpenter's tool.

He stepped closer. It was artificial! Someone had enclosed a gap between the two sides of the trunk with boards. They were wedged together perfectly but made up of five vertical sections.

"Rhett!" Shelley said in alarm. "I hear them. They're closing in."

"Turn the handle, Dad," Corwin said.

"Handle? What handle?"

Corwin stepped forward and reached for a piece of knotted wood in the artificial section. His fingers gripped the knot and turned. As he did this, Dee pushed on the surface.

Without even a squeak, the whole section swung inwards on unseen hinges to reveal a dimly lit interior.

"Quick!" Shelley hissed. "Get inside!"

She practically shoved the children in and placed an arm around Rhett. Without really thinking, he allowed himself to be guided inside a massive hollow trunk. He stood back against the wall and watched Shelley close the door. It shut with a distinct click.

Unexpectedly it had not become dark. Rhett turned and saw the reason why. The back of the trunk was open. He could see the grass outside and, further back, another tree trunk. All the lizard had to do was wander around the tree to see them from the other side!

He grabbed the fire extinguisher that he'd stuck in his backpack and stepped forward through the gap. His feet touched a pile of leaves and acorns. He studied the forest ahead. The adjacent tree was not covered in green leaves but stood bare and empty. Two other oaks nearby were also bare. It was as if the forest had gone from summer to winter within a few seconds.

He shivered and realised that a cold breeze was blowing on his cheeks.

"There was a latch on the inside that we closed." Shelley stood beside him and stared at the view. "The trees..."

'I know. They've lost their leaves and have you noticed how cold it has become?"

"And the beeping in my earrings has stopped," Shelley whispered.

"No, Mum," Dee said. "The original sound has returned." She had her arm around her brother and her eyes shone in excitement. "The one that led me to the monastery is back."

"But the girifa and the lizard?'

"They're on the other side of the portal, Dad," Dee said. "They can't get through."

"But where are we?"

"I'd say we're in the same place but have moved forward or perhaps backwards six months in time from summer to winter," Shelley said. "Dee's earring guided us to this tree."

"You're wrong, Mum," Dee said. "My earrings were telling me we were off course. Weren't yours?"

Shelley gasped. "They were. I remember. The beeps were becoming slower as if we were moving away from the correct path."

"We couldn't find the portal so it came to us," Corwin said in as matter-of-fact tone. "It would not allow us to be caught and you know why, don't you?"

"No," Rhett replied.

"Of course," Dee said. "If we had been caught, Corwin and me would cease to be for we would not have been born. Do you understand?"

Rhett stared at Shelley. He'd almost forgotten she was still really only a stranger and they hadn't even ... Oh hell. He flushed in embarrassment.

"I know it's hard," Shelley said and took his hand. "I hope you are not angry."

"Anything but," Rhett replied and kissed her firmly on the lips.

Dee grinned and Corwin glanced away with a look of distaste on his face. "Don't like that mushy stuff," he muttered. He did, though, smile when Shelley hugged him and placed a sloppy kiss on his cheek. There were other differences, too. It was getting colder and darker. They must have arrived late in the afternoon and, being winter, darkness would arrive soon. A brief survey around showed the same forest but one of bare trees with a carpet of dried leaves on the ground. When Rhett walked around the tree there was no door on the other side, just a wide flat trunk. Back inside the hollow trunk the door was still there with an old fashioned metal bolt that fitted in a grove to hold the door shut. He could also see metal hinges on the right hand side.

"So we can open it and go back?" he asked.

"I'd say so," Shelley replied. "I wouldn't though."

"I didn't intend to. This trunk is a good a place as any to stay. I think we should remain here until the morning."

*

Late that night and with the children fast asleep in the hollow trunk, Rhett realised Shelley wasn't there. In almost a panic, he jumped up and stepped into the darkness. Nearby he saw a torch light beam and Shelley appeared.

"Call of nature," she said and stood before him. "This must be an old forest."

"Why?"

"There are several hollow trunk trees. I thought..."

Rhett stared at the young woman standing there in the semi-darkness that fluctuated as moonlight shone through moving foliage overhead. His heart began to race. She looked so beautiful with long combed out hair and the small quiver of her chin. Even the slightly sweaty odour of her body was like an electrical bolt through his mind. Emotions, not felt for years, were generated. Something inside, perhaps those future thoughts made him want Shelley more than any human he had ever known. He wanted to hold her, protect her and become part of her life physically as well as emotionally.

She must have misinterpreted his body language for she hesitated and turned away. "It was a silly idea. There is nothing to prove the children are even related to us, anyway."

"Shut up!" Rhett whispered and seized her in an embrace so tight she gasped. Their emotional and bruising kiss and made their earlier encounter like a maiden aunt's peck.

"Not here," she whispered.

She took his hand and led him the few metres to another tree that had a dry sheltered space inside another triangular trunk. This one was only a meter high, though so she had to crawl inside. She did so, turned and shone the torch beam in his eyes.

"We don't want to be away from the children for too long," she said.

Without another word he slid in over her. Passions of the last few hours, or was it days or even years, came to a climax of frantic love making, a man and woman from different space-time but together in this lonely forest as if it was premeditated by the annals of history.

The minutes became almost an hour before an exhausted Shelley wriggled out, redressed in ruffled clothes, stood up and glanced at her watch.

"Oh my stars, the time!" She grabbed the torch and tore back to the other tree.

Rhett followed and grinned when he looked in the hollow interior over her shoulders. Dee was lying across the ground with an arm tucked over her brother's waist. Both were sound asleep.

Shelley smiled at Rhett and reached for her knapsack.

"Apple?" she asked in an innocent voice as if the last hour had never happened and held one out to him.

*

CHAPTER FIVE

It took Rhett a few seconds to orientate himself when he felt himself being awoken. He lay there with his eyes shut and tried to associate the smells tickling his nose, the scent of wood, burning methylated spirits and coffee.

"Daddy, wake up!" Dee was shaking his arm. "Something's happening."

Rhett jerked up and became fully alert.

He glanced around but everything appeared peaceful. Shelley was still asleep with her head on her backpack. Tiny blue flames were rising from their methylated spirits camp stove that Dee must have started up. The kettle bubbled above it. It was surprisingly snug in the hollow trunk but outside, rain tumbled down.

"It's started to rain?" he asked.

Dee stared at him, wide-eyed and nervous. "The door?"

Rhett turned to look at the door. It was still firmly shut and latched. "What about it?"

"It's shrinking!"

Rhett frowned and studied the door. There was enough light to see it quite clearly. It looked almost like an old fashioned church door with the top coming to a point. From this side there was a wooden frame around it that held the hinges and outer section of the latch. The door would now only come up to his chin. He thought back. When he originally walked through it he didn't have to bend his head.

"Oh hell!" he gasped.

Even as he watched it became smaller. Slowly but surely, the frame contracted. He reached forward but Dee grabbed his hand.

"No," she gasped. "You'll be sucked away!"

Because of her urgent tone, he hesitated. "What do you mean?"

Dee turned to Corwin. "Do it again," she said.

Corwin nodded and picked up a piece of bark from the floor. He looped it up so it hit the door as it dropped. There was a sort of slurp and the spot where the bark hit the wood vibrated in ripples like ones that would be created if something was thrown into still water. But there was more! A whisk of smoke spiralled up and the bark disappeared.

Afterwards, the door shrank at a faster rate.

"I kicked a bit of wood into it before," Corwin whispered. "The same thing happened and that's when it began to grow smaller."

"When it happened the first time another noise came back." Dee continued. "I'm sure there was a buzzing noise outside but it may have been from my earrings."

"No. I heard it, too." Corwin said.

"The portal's closing."

Rhett jumped in fright until he realised that it was Shelley who spoke. She was sitting up and staring at the door.

Within a minute it was only a metre tall and sliding inwards like balloon deflating. It was now half as big again... a mere thirty centimetres high... as big as a plate, a postage stamp before, with a pop, it disappeared.

"Portals have fail-safe mechanisms," Shelley said. "I think the girifa were trying to force it open from the other side with some electronic device. Our side shifted."

"Our side?"

"Yes. They would have succeeded in opening it from their side."

"But where to?"

"Probably the same place but at a different time. It could be anything from a day to a thousand years. Time cannot be measured in the fifth dimension."

"So they could be out there in the forest waiting for us?"

Shelley shook her head. "Oh they'll be in the forest but not in our time. They'll blunder around for hours trying to find us but we're here, not there." She smiled and glanced around. "And you both started breakfast for us?"

Dee nodded. "Corwin and I been awake for ages. I was going to let you sleep..." She frowned. "So what do we do now, Mum?"

"Go back to the monastery. I'm sure it'll still be there."

"But we wait for the rain to stop," Rhett said. "Even if we if go directly there, the journey will take a couple of hours."

He never said anything but doubt gnawed in his mind. What if there was no monastery? There was no way back and, with four of them, their food supplies would last for more than a few days. They could wander in an endless forest until they starved, got caught by aliens or even be attacked by wild animals.

"No," Shelley whispered and squeezed his hand. "We must survive. The laws of time-space have made that a certainty."

"And you remember all these things?"

"I do," Shelley whispered. "I think memories override my amnesia if they are necessary for our safety."

"You know this?"

"No but isn't it a logical conclusion and there's something else, too."

"The children?" Rhett asked.

"Yes. If we'd failed they would never have existed but they're here so we must succeed. Believe in yourself, Rhett. We'll make it." She reached out, slid her arms through his, kissed him on the cheek and bent down to kiss both the children. "We have each other and that makes me feel confident that everything will turn out okay."

*

After a wait of two hours while the rain tumbled down, Shelley suggested they move out. She said she could hear spasmodic beeps from her earrings but Dee said she could still hear a strong signal when she faced left outside the tree. This was probably the direction back to the monastery if, indeed, it existed in this new world.

They dressed the children warmly in oversized clothes and had a cold meal before setting off. Rhett glanced around at featureless forest. All the trees were bare with gnarled trunks and branches. The ground was covered in dead leaves and acorns with tufts of grass growing through. A watery sunlight flickered through the limbs and drips dropped from overhead branches. Without, Dee's navigation, he was sure they'd be lost within moments. He marked their tree and continued to cut small marks in trees as they walked along in case they ever needed to return.

The forest was hushed with the only noise being that of their feet crunching through the leaves. No birds called out and even the sound of the river had gone. Dee led with a confidence that Rhett didn't feel. There were so many things that could go wrong that even thinking about their situation made him shudder.

"A path," Dee said in a soft voice forty minutes later.

They stepped out onto a muddy track that came from their left and disappeared between the oaks to the right. Two water filled ruts showed in the mud. Rhett frowned and walked across to them. Some sort of vehicle had made the ruts. Skinny wheel tracks sunk several centimetres into the ground. The ruts crossed each other and showed where later vehicles had moved out of the original ruts onto more solid ground. Large flat footprints showed in a few soft spots.

"What do you make of all this?" he asked Shelley.

"It's created by a four wheeled wagon pulled by an upright creature with a long tail." Shelley pointed to a flat line between the footprints and stepped out between the footprints. Even by stretching her feet as far as she could there was no way she could step from one footprint to the next in one go. "It's big and heavy, I'd say heavier than the cart it was pulling. See how the footprints sink deeper into the ground than the wheel ruts?"

"Its got big toenails," Corwin said and pointed to two distinct footprints a few metres away. At the front of three toe prints, deep imprints dug into the ground.

"I don't like it," Shelley whispered. "I don't know any creature that would leave footprints like this."

"The track's going the way we need to head, though," Dee said. "My beep is now almost a constant buzz."

"So we'll follow this track but stay in the trees," Rhett glanced around. "Let's cover our own footprints we made."

A broken branch with twigs made a reasonable rake so they soon covered evidence of being there to all except the most concerning eyes.

Afterwards, they walked back into the trees and followed the path. The ground under the trees was still leaf strewn and was easier to walk on than the muddy path would have been anyway.

Another hour slipped by and Rhett became more worried. If they were in the same place but at a different time, they should be close to the hill that the monastery was built on by now. But the land was still flat and forest featureless. The track curved around larger trees and a few dips but, otherwise went straight through the forest.

"We need to stop, have a rest and have something to eat," Shelley said. "The children are getting tired." She wiped a hand over her sweaty forehead. "I am too."

"Someone's coming!" Dee gasped. "Listen!"

In the distance behind, Rhett heard a creaking noise and the slurp of wheels moving through mud.

"Quick!" He grabbed both children's hands and after checking that Shelley was with them, dived though the trees and behind yet another gigantic oak.

They squatted down, the children looking scared and Shelley apprehensive. Rhett signalled for them to remain still. He lay on his stomach, wriggled forward and found a spot where he could see the track ahead from beneath an oversized root.

An arm went through his and he glanced sideways to see Shelley beside him. She moved closer so she could also see through the gap beneath the root. Another hand grabbed his. Dee squeezed his outside hand while Corwin cuddled in under Shelley's protection.

They waited.

*

The creature that appeared was the strangest Rhett had ever seen in the flesh. It did however jolt his memory from high school days when he remembered descriptions of prehistoric dinosaurs. It towered upright on two hind legs about four metres high, had an almost beak like nose, darting green lizard eyes, a long neck and short forelegs. Hitched to it's middle were two wooden bars connected to a wooden wagon with a canvas top that wouldn't go amiss in an old cowboy movie. The creature's long tail dragged along the ground between the front wheels.

"Oh my stars," Dee whispered. "What is it?"

"I think it's a tsintaosaurus, a grass eating dinosaur that became extinct on Earth millions of years ago."

"And there's the wagon master," Shelley whispered.

An old man with a massive beard and dressed in old-fashioned clothes, appeared from the other side of the wagon. He frowned and spoke.

"Why are you slowing, Zarleg?" he asked.

Rhett froze for he could understand the words. He felt two hands squeeze his arms and was sure that either Shelley or Dee had made it possible for him to understand the stranger's speech.

The creature replied with a guttural grunt.

"So you smell something, Zarleg?" The old guy laughed. "Not fresh grass again? I'm afraid your imagination is getting the better of you, my friend. Unfortunately, there will be only hay and acorns for you tonight."

He listened as the tsintaosaurus tilted its head sideways and grunted again.

"You're saying, Krass that there's something alive and of my sort nearby?"

Krass continued to hold a conversation with the creature who grunted or hissed at appropriate times. It stretched its head down and stopped walking

"Warm blooded animals, you say?" Krass screwed up his nose and glanced towards the tree where Rhett and the others remained hidden. "Humans?"

The creature called Zarleg stretched its neck up again and turned.

Rhett froze for the darting eyes became a stare that looked directly at him a second before moving on. Finally it bent its head down beside the man and gave a series of low grunts,

"They're in physical form and conscious?" Krass said. "But that's impossible. You know that the only warm blooded creatures in this country are the lost souls in deep hibernation." He sighed. "This is the last shipment of plasma from the hospital. Without more, our keepsakes will be dead within a week."

Zarleg turned and again stared at the tree where Rhett and the others were hiding. It raised its head and growled.

"Cut it out, Zarleg," Krass said. "You're making me nervous...What? They're scared, too? Two minors, a female and a male."

Rhett shuddered. How did the tsintaosaurus know that?

Krass continued to talk as if there was a two-way conversation "I see... They've come from beyond the realm...Oh, poppycock. You've been listening to the prophets of the old religion for so long, it's warping your mind."

"I think he can understand the creature's grunts," Shelley whispered

Krass continued to talk "If you say so, Zarleg." He walked around to their side of the wagon and stepped cautiously towards them. "Come out," he called. "Why do you hide like cowardly lizards?"

"I'll stand," Rhett whispered and stood up.

However, Shelley and the children also rose beside him.

"We are here," Rhett said as he stepped out with his hands held wide.

Krass shrank back and ran a tongue over his lips. Zarleg just turned his head sideways and bent forward until its face was mere metres from Rhett. Its tongue flickered and a gurgling sound came from its throat.

"You came here though a portal to help the five, didn't you?" Krass continued.

"We came to rescue our children." Shelley replied.

Krass looked at Zarleg who studied Rhett, Shelley and the two children in turn. Dee placed an arm around Corwin's shoulders and held the creature's eyes. "I trust them both," she whispered.

Krass gave a sort of bow. "Zarleg also trusts you, young human maiden and invites you all to ride with us."

Rhett nodded and hand in hand with the others, stepped forward.

"We know of no five." Shelley said when they reached the wagon. "Who are they?"

"The five humans who have become lost souls but will die when their bodies starve. We have our last supply of plasma for them." Krass smiled slightly. "Careful that you don't knock over the plasma bags hanging from the roof when you climb aboard. It'll be a tight fit but beats walking. Come nightfall, it'll be raining again and cold, that's for sure."

He walked around the rear of the wagon and held the canvas flap aside.

*

Darkness had dropped over the forest when Krass called Zarleg to a halt. He turned to face Rhett and the others at the back of the wagon. "It is too difficult to travel at night. The last thing we need is a broken axle. Also Zarleg wants his supper."

Everyone clamoured out and, within minutes, a small lean-to tent was attached to the side of the wagon, a campfire lit and slices of meat with vegetables cooked. The smell made Rhett realise how hungry he was. Krass only had two plates and a couple of mugs so fingers came to play as the children ate enthusiastically.

"What's the meat?" Shelley asked as she chewed on a tiny bone.

"A variety of pterosaurs," Krass replied. "No, it's not the massive one flying in some of the other continents. These have a metre wingspan and have been domesticated for hundreds of years for both their meat and eggs."

"Another cold blooded creature?" Rhett asked.

"All the living species on this world are cold blooded, from the smallest lizard to the ruling girifa, the reptilian equivalent of humanity."

"We know about them," Rhett said.

"But you're human?" Shelley asked.

Krass shut one eye, stroked his beard and stared at her. "I'm the exception that proves the rule." He laughed. "I was found as a baby and brought up by my adopted girifa parents. Whether I had natural immunity from the holocaust or arrived from the overworld, I don't know but I have spent forty years searching for humans and helping where I can."

"What is this holocaust you speak of?"

Krass frowned. "You did come from far away didn't you? It was the last big war between the girifa and animals on this world and by all accounts was a brutal affair. In the end the reptilian girifa developed biological weapons that attacked warm-blooded creatures. Every animal and bird died out within a decade. Since then, only girifa and reptiles have lived here."

"How awful," Shelley gasped. "When did this happen?"

"When I was a toddler sixty-nine years ago. I'm seventy-one now."

"And the five lost souls in hibernation?" Shelley continued.

"I have many girifa friends in this remote land. Most of them prefer to live in the warmer tropical climate closer to the equator. Two months back, one of the villagers approached me and said they found five humans in the forest. They were unconscious but still alive. I've managed to get ancient plasma blood from the ruins but this is the last supply."

"The ruins?" Shelley queried.

"One of the last human cities that was abandoned after the holocaust. Most of it has returned to forest but some of the more substantial buildings survive. The hospital I mentioned has its own solar energy and deep freeze vaults that contained this plasma. I think it was protected over the years because the vaults are too cold for the girifa to enter."

"And you just found these vaults?" Shelley sounded sceptical.

"No, one of the five told me where to go."

"You said they were unconscious," Rhett cut in.

"Aye, but their souls float around."

"Like tiny yellow balls," Shelley asked.

Krass frowned. "Yes. Do you know them?"

"They're identities. I was one too."

"So how come you're alive and here now?" the old man asked. "The five I look after cannot return to their bodies. When their bodies starve, they will die."

"They must be the original species. In my case I carried all the components within myself to rebuild my physical body. It was the only way to travel huge distances through space before space portals were discovered."

"You've lost me there, Shelley," Krass muttered. "I'm not into this overworld stuff. All I know is that I need to get this plasma back within a couple of days or my five will die." He sighed. "I thought I had enough the first time but had to make this second trip. This last lot is all there is. When it is used …" He shrugged and turned his eyes away.

"That's why we're here," Dee cried. "It all makes sense. It fits in with everything else, too."

"What do you mean, Dee?" Rhett asked.

Dee bit on her lip and flushed. "I didn't like to say."

"It's okay," Shelley said. "Remember we share everything now."

Dee nodded. "The hum in my earrings stopped when Krass's wagon arrived."

"But there's no portal here," Rhett whispered.

"I know." Dee was almost in tears. "I thought it'd come back but it hasn't."

"And yours?" Rhett glanced at Shelley.

"I've heard no sound. My signals were never as strong as Dee's anyway." Shelley placed an arm around Dee to comfort her. "I think she could be right. It is too much of a coincident that we just happened to be in the forest here when Krass a came by."

"Like everything else," Dee said. "You found Daddy, I found you both, we rescued Corwin and now we're here with Krass."

"Are gods are pulling our strings?" Krass asked.

"Something in space-time is operating," Shelley whispered. "Perhaps it could be called a god, Krass." She stood up and held her hands out to the fire. "Come on, I'll help clean up and then you two children are off to sleep. I think it's going to be a long day tomorrow."

*

CHAPTER SIX

All through the morning, Zarleg plodded along at about five kilometres and hour, the wagon wheels oozed through the mud and the wagon passengers spent their time sitting on the backboard or walking along beside him. The tsintaosaurus accepted them all and before long he was grunting away in response to the children's chatter.

"We'll be out of the forest in an hour," Corwin said as he sat swinging his legs from the backboard after they'd set off again after a lunch break.

"Will we?" Rhett replied. "Did Krass tell you that?"

The little boy looked up. "No... Zarleg. He also told me that not long afterwards we will come to the castles."

Rhett grinned. "You say castles?"

"Yes. There's a big one up the mountain and a little one at the bottom. That's where the lost souls are."

"And what's up in the big castle?"

Corwin shrugged. "Krass is too old to walk up all the steps so Zarleg hasn't been there."

"Sounds similar to the steps we came down," Dee added. She stood behind the pair clinging to the wagon frame with one hand while she munched on an apple type fruit with the other.

Rhett glanced to her. "And you talk to Zarleg too?"

Dee screwed her nose up and wriggled her finger around her ear as if to say it was just her brother's fantasy that he could speak to the tsintaosaurus.

However, almost to the dot an hour later, the forest came to an abrupt stop and their track continued through grassland with distant hills rising beyond the plain. Dee, who was now walking between Rhett and Shelley frowned and shaded her eyes from the sun.

"What is it?" Shelley asked.

"I recognise the hills. This is near the village where I lived." She stared at Rhett. "But it can't be. There were no creatures like Zarleg where I lived, only horses and cows." She frowned, clapped a hand over her right ear and broke into a smile. "My beeper has started. Perhaps we're heading back to the monastery where I found you."

Like Corwin earlier in the day, her prediction proved to be correct. When they moved closer to the hills, Rhett spotted white towers on a pinnacle sticking out from a larger hill. He couldn't remember the hill but this particular pinnacle looked familiar.

Shelley came up and slipped a hand through his. "It is the

monastery. My earring is working now, too. We've found our way back."

*

Dee wasn't sure whether the village they arrived at was one she knew or not. This wasn't surprising for all that remained were broken sections of road, a row of crumpled stone fences and twenty or so chimneys sticking up through grass and creeper. Several bushy trees could have been hedgerows and rusty circular frames were all that remained of water tanks. Tall spindly fruit trees grew in an unnatural row and a nearby stream held the stone foundations of what would have been a bridge large enough to drive a wagon across.

Today, though, they had to ford the stream before entering the village itself.

"The whole land is like this," Krass said. "When animal life was killed, the girifa attempted to move in. However, the cold winters made most of them drop into hibernation unless they wore especially designed clothing for warmth. After several years they all shifted north to a more tropical climate."

"North?" Rhett asked. "So we're in the southern hemisphere?"

Krass nodded. "Does it make any difference?"

"Not really, I lived in the southern hemisphere of Earth but the vast majority of the humans lived in the northern hemisphere." Rhett turned to Dee. "So you recognise nothing about this place?"

"Only the hills. There were stone bridges built over streams near most villages."

"Three kilometres to go," Krass said. "Zarleg will make it in about half an hour."

The monastery now stood out ahead while behind it, the hillside rose dark green and ominous. Rhett glanced at Shelley who shrugged. Like her, he wanted to go faster but the old man and plodding tsintaosaurus continued at a leisurely pace as if time didn't matter. In this world, it probably didn't.

"Look!" Corwin yelled and pointed into the sky.

Two yellow balls, like tiny balloons dropped down before them.

"Loretta and Irene," Krass said. "These two always come out to meet me. They're the younger girls in the deep sleep." He shrugged. "It's a guess though."

"So you talk to them?" Shelley asked.

"Me? I guess you could call it talking."

The balls dropped and hovered above like pulsing lights. Zarleg rose up and gave a guttural growl before turning to lower his head by Krass. He grunted, raised his head and grunted at the hovering balls.

"They're afraid of you," Krass said. "I told him to tell Loretta and Irene that you're real humans from the overworld who may be able to help."

Shelley nodded and held an opened hand out before her. She waited while one ball came closer like a timid child. "Come on," Shelley coaxed. "You have to touch me if you wish to communicate."

She grabbed Rhett's hand. "This is Rhett, my companion and these are my children, Dee and Corwin."

One ball hovered closer while the other stayed back as if it was ready to protect the front one if necessary.

"Hold your hand out like me," Shelley whispered to Rhett. "Look directly at the closest one and smile. They probably can't hear me yet but they can certainly read our body language."

"You need not be afraid of us," Dee called out. She stepped in front of Shelley and stood on tiptoes, reached the closest ball and cupped her fingers gently around it. At the same time she touched Rhett's arm.

"Nell's dead." A sobbing voice filled Rhett's mind. *"Krass took too long to get back. Nell's dead and Fran is so weak her identity just rolls on the bed beside her body. Please come quickly."*

Shelley turned to Krass and repeated the message. The old man frowned but never hesitated. He turned to Zarleg. "You need to get there as fast as you can, my friend." He turned back. "Get in the wagon otherwise you'll be left behind."

Rhett lifted Corwin and Dee up; Shelley followed and, unexpectedly so did the two identities, which the balls really were. Krass slung himself up on Zarleg, clung to the strap across his back and glanced back.

"Hang on!" he cried.

The pondering reptile bent forward so its forelegs touched the ground and galloped. The wagon creaked, bumped and practically flew along the track. Trees flew by in a blur and at one point; there was an almighty crunch when the wagon sideswiped a branch. Rhett grabbed Corwin and held him close while Shelley managed to stop Dee from toppling out the back. Backpacks, sacks, kitchen utensils and everything else not tied down, crashed onto the floor and the canvas ballooned up and flapped out from the framework. The two identities sort sanctuary within Shelley and Dee's shirt tops.

But the wagon was solid and remained in one piece as the tsintaosaurus roared and bounded forward at a phenomenal speed. Soon it was gasping. Clouds of condensation puffed from his nostrils, saliva dripped from his mouth and his gigantic tongue hung out the side of its mouth as it raced on.

Dee screamed for Zarleg's massive green tail swung up above

the wagon and wagged like a tormented cat's tail in front of her. A moment later a building, similar in shape to the monastery appeared ahead. Zarleg, with the flapping, creaking wagon still behind bounded through an archway, into a cobblestone courtyard.

He stopped, lay down on his tummy with his eyes shut and sides heaving, exhausted. Krass patted his neck and climbed down.

"This is the Lower Monastery. Come on." He ran through a doorway and up a set of steps inside.

*

The room that they entered was modern with electric lighting and the five humans, all young women dressed in modern but exotic looking clothes, lying on metallic slabs above which were hung the plastic plasma bags. Plastic tubing went down to needles, inserted into veins in the patient's lower arms. Every plasma bag was empty or contained just a few millimetres of liquid inside. Two young women were a ghastly white and no sign of movement in their bodies.

" I don't understand," Krass whispered. " I know I was a little late but..."

"*Five days, Krass. You said you'd take ten days at the outside. It was fifteen.*" Rhett heard the voice in his mind without an identity touching him.

"I'm sorry, Loretta," Krass whispered. "It was difficult."

"We need the plasma," Shelley cut in. She reached the closest woman and felt for a pulse.

Rhett followed. Two were dead but the others he examined had weak pulses. He discovered that the third slab contained Loretta's unconscious body. Her identity hovered above the thin body.

"*I'm okay. Feed the others first,*" she said.

Even Dee and Corwin helped the adults bring up the plasma bags and replace the empty ones above the unconscious women. Within moments the languishing identities brightened and flew around the room. Rhett glanced at Shelley as they examined the unconscious women. They were in their twenties and if it wasn't for the gaunt bodies and faces would be attractive women. Loretta was a blonde, Irene a freckled redhead and Sarine an Asian woman. One dead woman was a black African the other, of Chinese ancestry.

Shelley connected plasma to the last surviving patient and stood back frowning. "Did you try to awaken them, Krass?" she asked.

The old man nodded. "It was a disaster. Whenever, they came even close to waking up, their bodies went into violent spasms that only retreated when their souls left again.

"*That's true,*" one of the identities added. "*If it wasn't for Krass we'd all be dead by now. He rescued our bodies from our escape pod. I think he thought we were ghosts when we communicated with him.*"

Krass smiled. "I must admit it took me a while to realise what you were."

"Where are you from?" Shelley asked.

Loretta's voice replied. "*We have no idea. None of us can remember anything except waking up in the forest and looking down at our bodies lying inside this pod shaped vehicle. We worked out everything else by trial and error. It was obvious that our bodies were starving and we would only live a week or so if we didn't get help.*"

"Loretta spoke to me." Krass grinned. "Before she did that I didn't have a strand of grey hair..."

"*You were no different,*" Loretta continued.

"Yeah well. Zarleg convinced me the lost souls... oops I mean identities were just advanced humans and not figments of my imagination. I brought them here and I guess you know the rest of the story."

Rhett grinned. "I know what it's like. When Shelley arrived at my place I was terrified."

"You were not," Shelley cut in. "I was the scared one. I didn't even have clothes..." She briefly told everyone about how they met.

"*But you changed back?*" Rhett began to recognise the identities' voices. This was Loretta speaking.

"All identities can change back," Shelley said. "Some species have learned to replenish themselves without using their physical bodies but they all have them."

"*So why can't we?*" Irene seemed to have an Irish accent.

"Residual from the holocaust," Krass said. "Airborne spores still attack animal species and ultimately kill them."

"But we're fine," Rhett replied. "I don't even have a cold."

Krass shrugged. "I guess like myself, you're immune."

"All of us?" Shelley whispered.

"*It could be that you're ancestors of human survivors with genes that aren't affected by the spores on this planet.*" Loretta said.

"*In space-time, your worlds could be centuries ahead of ours.*" Irene's identity pulsed. "*This talk doesn't help us though.*"

"True," Shelley replied. "I think we need to check out the top monastery as soon as possible."

*

Krass made two simple dignified coffins and Zarleg dug two

holes in the ancient cemetery found beyond the outer walls of the Lower Monastery so the two bodies could be buried. Even though Rhett, Shelley and the children never knew the dead women, it was a moving occasion with the three remaining dignities hovering over their shoulders as they helped lowered the coffins into the ground. Krass read two eloquent passages from an ancient book he produced from a trunk in his wagon. Afterwards, Zarleg used a back paw to fill the graves in and Krass placed a circle of stones on each grave.

"I guess you know The Old Religion had this symbol signifying the cycle of life," Krass explained.

"I'm sorry, I don't," Shelley replied. "My memories are fragmented."

Krass shrugged. "At times like this, ancient words are often helpful. I think our friends are as worried about their own mortality as the death of their friends. It is them we should now help."

"Of course." Rhett studied the old man and perceived that the words showed a genuine concern for the quivering identities. If a ball of energy could display emotion these little balls did so now.

As they headed back Zarleg lowered his head next to Krass and gave a low grunt.

"Don't look around but we're being watched by a thousand eyes," Krass whispered. "Just keep walking and show no urgency or fear."

Rhett reached out, found Dee's hand in his and noticed she had grabbed Corwin's hand, too.

Shelley linked her arm through his and caught his eyes. "The girifa have arrived," she whispered.

Rhett could see nothing unusual. He continued to talk about nothing in particular but increased his pace slightly. The two hundred metres to the archway ahead seemed like two kilometres with even Zarleg walking faster as his tail dragged along the ground.

"They'll let us get back," Krass whispered, "The girifa have respect for the dead and will not interrupt the funeral service. If, however, they suspect it is over, they will attack us."

Rhett turned slightly and gasped. About three hundred metres out, two lines of warriors encircled them, huge bald creatures who held long spears and circular shields. They were probably of both sexes but this was difficult to ascertain for creatures descended from reptiles did not feed young on milk so the females had no breasts. The shorter ones with larger posteriors were most likely to be female. The warriors all had bronze coloured skin and wore tunics that hung from the shoulders. The only sign of any rank was in ringlets that several wore around their necks. A warrior that stood ten metres in front of the rest had four silver ringlets and a larger shield than the others.

"The big chief," Krass hissed, "Be very careful. For him to stand before his warriors is significant."

Zarleg growled and turned towards the new arrivals. He lowered his head like a stalking cat and moved his head towards the warrior chief.

"Can we help?" Loretta asked.

"I think they realise the funeral service is over. We'll need to run. On three, I want you identities to head for that head guy and his two offshoots. They're the ones with two neck rings. Fly right though them and create havoc. Zarleg, ignore the chiefs and stop the closest line from throwing their spears. Just trample as many as you can then head back. Don't do anything rash. You only need to stop the first attack."

Zarleg turned his head and growled as if he disagreed.

"No," Krass insisted. "Not even your thick hide will be enough if a hundred turn on you. " He turned to Rhett and the others. "On three, run, count to six, swerve to the left together, count five swerve back again and head straight for the archway. Three, six , five. Get it?"

Rhett squeezed the hands he was holding. Dee trembled and Shelley stepped in behind the children. "We're ready."

Krass nodded. "One, two... Three!" he hissed.

They did ... just as all hell broke loose!

*

Visions of running children beside him filled Rhett's mind. He grabbed and lifted Corwin as he ran. On the count of six he swerved to the left just as a spear imbedded itself in the ground ... right where he would have been if he hadn't swerved. Another five paces to the right... Dee stumbled with a scream. He hesitated, but saw Shelley had lifted her up. They swerved back again... Two spears hit the ground on each side and sprayed dust up. The archway was straight ahead. Rhett still had Corwin in his arms as he gasped for oxygen and ran. But where were Shelley and Dee? He turned and saw the pair stagger.

Two identities were with him.

"Help Shelley," Irene cried. *"I'll guide Corwin in."*

Rhett turned, caught the flash of something and bent down. Another spear hissed across his shoulder. He was with Shelley and Dee. In a massive burst of adrenaline, he grabbed one under each arm and continued forward.

"Almost there!" he heard Krass gasp.

He reached the archway, almost threw the pair in his arms forward and turned. Zarleg had arrived. Krass dived to the right, seized an axe from an adjacent wall clamp and chopped through a restraining rope.

A wooden door dropped from above, three identities flew in and another spear caught the corner of his eyes. Rhett dived left; something jarred his shoulder and flung him sideways. Pain, more terrible than he'd ever felt before shot through his right side. He reached up to steady himself, staggered and fell. Something wet his shirt. It was black and gooey... blood. His blood!

"Rhett!" Shelley screamed.

His last blurry recollection was hearing the door hit the ground with a thud and feeling warm arms encircle his own.

"You're hurting..." he started to cry out but the world began to spin as he collapsed beside Shelley. He saw her shocked horrified expression as she stared at his shoulder.

"Help me, Krass," he heard her screaming as if she was a million kilometres away. "A spear's gone through Rhett's shoulder."

The world switched off and he remembered no more.

*

CHAPTER SEVEN

Shelley stared in horror at Rhett. Blood was pouring from beneath a wooden spear imbedded beneath his right shoulder blade. He lay back, unconscious on the courtyard stones.

"Rhett!" she screamed. Ignoring the blood soaking into her clothes, she hugged him close and glanced up. "Do something!"

For an elderly man, Krass was surprisingly strong. He stooped down, lifted Rhett into his hands and carried him through to the room where the identities' bodies were lying. He laid him sideways on one of the empty metallic slabs and held gauze to the wound.

Shelley paled. The spear had gone right through Rhett's shoulder and protruded out his back. The end consisted of an ugly barb. If it was pulled out, these spikes would cause more damage than when the spear originally went in. The bleeding was reduced to a dribble but he was pale with blue lips and erratic breaths.

"Mum," Dee cried. "I feel strange."

"Daddy will be okay. He..." Shelley turned and suppressed a scream. Both Dee and Corwin were transparent... she could see right through them! Even as she watched they both became fainter.

"*I believe there's a conflict of space-time.*" Sarine, the third and quietest identity said. "*How are you related to Rhett and the children?*"

"Dee and Corwin are our children."

"*From your original world?*"

"Well no."

The identity landed on Shelley's shoulder. "*Even though I have no memory of my past life I believe I have studied the space-time phenomenon in relation to parallel universes and human life. Not only Rhett's life is in danger but also your children are affected.*"

Shelley stared at Rhett then onto the children. Without warning she erupted into tears that rolled down her cheeks. "We never knew we had children until..." In stuttering gasps between the sobs she told Sarine and the others about how they met Dee. "So if Rhett dies the children will disappear too?"

"*If he dies now you will never have given birth to Dee and Corwin. His and your own future as it would have been will be destroyed. This includes your children's lives.*"

"Please help him," Shelley sobbed.

An arm guided her to a nearby couch. "We will help, Shelley," Krass said. "I believe we can succeed. We'll need to hook him to a supply of plasma, remove the spear and sew up the wound."

"*And we'll do what we can to help,*" Loretta added.

"How?" Shelley wept.

"*It is true we cannot physically touch anything but we can exert other forces. Have faith and trust in us.*"

While they talked, Krass clipped one of the spare plasma bags up and inserted a needle into Rhett's left arm. He brought out a bowl of warm water, added disinfectant from a brown bottle and gently rubbed the edges of the wounds around the spear.

"I'm sorry," Shelley whispered as she wiped her eyes. "How can I help?"

"Keep applying pressure to the gauze where the spear entered him. That will stop more bleeding. I have to go and find a saw."

Shelley nodded but never asked why he needed one. She held the gauze to the wound and gazed up. Both Dell and Corwin were slumped on an adjacent couch, asleep and still a ghostly transparent in appearance.

"*The transfusion of plasma is helping,*" Loretta said. "*I believe Rhett's pulse is more stable now. His body has gone through the shock phase and is assisting rather than fighting his recovery.*"

Shelley just bit on her lower lip and nodded. She knew that the worse was still to come. They had to remove the spear but how could they stop the wounds from bleeding? He'd already lost so much blood she doubted if the plasma could replace any more lost quickly enough to save his life. She shook her head as more tears squeezed out the edge of her eyes. Three lives! She'd lose the children, too. It wasn't fair. Rhett and them had never hurt a soul in their lives. They didn't deserve to die!

"*It's going to be okay,*" Sarine whispered. "*He's over the worst. Did you know love actually radiates energy?*"

Shelley shook her head.

"*Well it does. High frequency gamma waves are radiated between living beings who love each other. Our scientists actually isolated the signals and have produced artificial signals to help seriously ill patients recover from accidents or war wounds like Rhett's.*"

"And you remember that?"

"*Like with yourself, it seems that flashes of memories return when they are relevant to my situation.*"

Krass returned with a small cross saw. He explained what he was about to do and stared at the identities. "When the spear comes out, the next few seconds are crucial. Are you sure what you told me will work?"

"*We are confident,*" Sarine replied.

Krass took Shelley's hand. "Go and look after the children," he said. "It is important they have you with them."

"But I want to help."

"I know but you can do no more at the moment." His eyes linked on her. "Please, trust us, my friend. I will not be working alone."

"But identities can do nothing. I know. I've been one."

"Please," Krass whispered and guided her over to the couch by the children.

Shelley sat between and hugged the children. She found their bodies were warm but as soft as jelly and the transparent appearance extended to all their exposed skin. "May the faith of a thousand worlds work for us," she whispered and tried to slow her pounding heart.

*

Krass cut through the protruding barb and poured water over the fractured end to wash away sawdust. While two identities hovered nearby he turned Rhett slightly so he was lying diagonally across the slab with the spear protruding over the edge. He glanced up, gave a brief nod and seized it.

He pulled and the spear came out, along with a fountain of blood. Krass, now with his arms soaked in blood, stood back.

"Do something!" Shelley screamed, sprang to her feet and rushed forward.

However, powerful hands seized her and held on tightly.

"Let me go!" Shelley howled as she flung her arms out and kicked. "You can't just let him bleed to death."

"Just look." Krass refused to relax his hold.

She had no option but to obey. She glanced up and saw an identity fly directly into the fountain of blood. The gush became a mere trickle when the ball 'sat' on the wound. A second identity came in under Rhett's back and stopped the blood flow underneath in a similar way. Finally, the pair flew away to expose two large scar tissues that covered the wounds. The last identity now flew over the top wound, changed shape to that of an elongated pencil, even down to a pointed end. The point touched the top scab.

Shelley could see the skin sort of sizzle and melt as the pencil-shaped identity pierced the skin and burrowed in. For a moment it looked like a spear of light that turned from yellow to red and finally black.

But more happened! The pencil came out the other side. As the top section disappeared the skin rolled back and coagulated to form only a faintest of scars. Finally the identity sort of popped out Rhett's back and the wound there came together leaving no mark at all.

"We cauterise the wound," Sarine said. *"Luckily no major organs were hit. It will be tender for a few days but, otherwise, Rhett will be as good as new."*

There was another sensation as the two children in Shelley's arms became solid, Dee opened her eyes and stared up at her. "Daddy will be fine, Mum," she whispered.

"Can we go back to the beach one day, Mummy?" Corwin added as he, too, opened his eyes.

"What beach, Sweetheart?" Shelley asked.

"I dreamt that we were all walking along a beautiful beach with breakers crashing on white sand."

Dee gasped. "I did, too. Two other kids who called Daddy, Uncle Rhett were there as well."

"Riversdale," Shelley whispered. "Those two children were your cousins." She smiled At Krass and the identities. "The dream must be a good sign."

"Yes. It's a future memory, I'd say," Sarine said. *"The fact that both of you had this dream is a good sign."*

"Now the other spear," Krass muttered.

"What other spear," Shelley asked.

"The one Zarleg got in his tail. Didn't you notice?" Krass laughed. "Don't worry. It hardly hurt him but don't tell him I said that."

After making sure Rhett was as comfortable as possible, Shelley followed the others downstairs and saw Krass beside the tsintaosaurus who had a spear protruding from his tail. When Krass gave the spear and a yank, it came flying out along with a small amount of blood. An identity landed on the wound and within moments it was cauterised but Zarleg continued to let his tail drag along the ground.

"Oh don't be a boob, Zarleg, it had to come out." Krass turned to Shelley and the children beside her. "His hide is like armour plating but he likes to moan when things go wrong."

Zarleg's neck was out of reach so Dee and Corwin ran up and hugged his front leg to comfort him. He lowered his head, gave a soft moan and sort of rolled his eyes as if he loved the attention.

"Don't give him too much sympathy," Krass said. "He's getting soft in his old age."

"If it wasn't for him we could have been caught out there," Dee said.

"Possibly," Krass admitted. "Anyway, I'd better go up to the top parapet and check on the enemy."

"We already have," Loretta said. *"The girifa have retreated a hundred metres and look as if they're setting up a camp."*

Krass pouted. "Typical," he muttered. "They know they can't breech our walls so will begin a siege. This brings us back to my original problem. With only three of you identities the plasma will last a while longer but ultimately it will run out. We have a bore here, so water is not a problem but our food will also eventually run out."

"How long will they stay out there?" Shelley asked.

"Days, weeks even months. It depends on whether they are just an isolated raiding party or part of a larger tribe under orders to imprison us."

"Because we're human?" Shelley whispered.

"I guess. I was tolerated because I was a loner but more humans here could be seen as a threat. The local girifa are also superstitious. If they think you arrived from another world they could read it as a sign of some future catastrophe. In their eyes the only solution to the problem is to kill us all."

"You too?" Shelley asked.

"If you are from the dark world as they call it and I've befriended you, I have lost my neutrality and don't deserve to live." The old man gave a whisk of a smile. "I'm glad we met, though. It was getting a mite lonely with only Zarleg for company."

*

Shelley tried to sleep that night but there were too many thoughts going through her mind. Rhett had awoken a few hours earlier but was still weak and sore. He'd drifted off again and the children were also asleep. After just lying for almost an hour, she slipped on an overcoat and walked up a flight of stone steps to the parapet. As far as she could see outside were campfires, forty or more in every direction except the hill on which the other monastery stood.

"Aye it's bad, lass. Worse than I first thought."

Shelley jumped in fright but relaxed when she turned to see Krass standing at the top of the stairs. "The fires?"

"They keep the fires stoked on these cooler night. They'd be lethargic out there but still alert. Guards will be wearing thermal clothing to keep their blood warm." He stepped forward and rested his hands on the parapet wall. "More have arrived, too. This is a major siege, I'm afraid."

"Just to get us?"

"It's what you and the identities represent. They're scared and are being feed rumours from someone else to fuel their superstitions."

"Who?"

Krass stared at her. "If you could travel through space-time, why couldn't the girifa of your time also do the same? Weren't you at war with them?"

Shelley nodded. "I think so but how did you know?"

"Loretta and the other identities may not have come from your world or time but their situation was similar. With modern transportation it is no longer an advantage being in a remote corner of the known universe."

"And where are we?"

"I'm nor sure but it could possibly be Earth."

Shelley gasped. "But Earth does not have reptilian creatures like Zarleg on it. All the higher living creatures are warm blooded animals or birds."

"Yes," Krass whispered. "But what if Earth Alpha is not the real Earth but a parallel substitute?"

"What do you mean?"

"Animal life including humans evolved over millions of years. Am I right?"

Shelley nodded.

"What if this was not the natural course of evolution but the reptilian line of life matured instead? What would we have?"

"Girifa?"

"Yes and domesticated reptiles like Zarleg. There are others, you know; reptiles that provide us with commercial meat or lay eggs that we eat."

"Rhett said there were once dinosaurs on Earth Alpha but they became extinct."

"But if they didn't?"

"So animals and humans are the freaks of nature and not the result of natural evolution?"

"That's what the girifa civilisations of your time believe. In their opinion, a cosmos without humanity is a return to what should have been."

"That's militant propaganda," Shelley snapped. "At other times humans and girifa lived happily together."

"And still do somewhere out there." Krass gazed up at the star-studded sky. "Unfortunately, that is not the case here."

"So what do you suggest we do, Krass?"

"Wait for or go to a portal."

Shelley frowned. "What do you mean?"

"From what you told me, you already went through a portal inside that oak tree. If you were meant to go though a portal, isn't it a possibility that one will arrive here so you can continue your journey?"

"With Loretta, Irene and Sarine?"

"Yes."

"And the 'go' bit of your statement?"

"Your theory that it could be waiting at that top monastery."

"And how do we know?"

"I would ask the identities to help but they're still weak."

"Go on..."

"You know what you need to do, Shelley," Krass replied and disappeared back down the stairs without another word.

Shelley gasped. Of course, she could revert to being an identity and go up herself. But how? Originally, a computer had helped her become one to escape impending death but there was no computer here now. Deep in thought she wandered back inside and climbed into bed. Rhett was still asleep and she soon found her eyes closing with the unanswered questions still on her mind.

*

"It's okay to wake up, Shelley, I'm here to help." Loretta's voice filled her mind.

Shelley felt light-headed and disorientated as she forced her eyes open from a deep sleep. She was bouncing against the bedroom ceiling and could see the room below in the early dawn light. Rhett was lying sideways on the bed with his arms around a woman. Her lassitude was replaced by jealousy and anger as adrenaline pulsed through her veins.

"Oh Shelley," laughed Loretta. *"Look closer."*

Almost in tears, Shelley looked again and found herself dropping. She managed to stop the sudden fall but found herself beside the bed and the woman. Her glower turned to a gasp when the hussy turned in her sleep and flung an arm out. Oh my stars, it wasn't a stranger, it was herself lying beside Rhett. Anger, turned to embarrassment as she turned and noticed a pulsing ball floating beside her.

"Loretta?" The one word sounded normal but she knew she had not spoken. Identities don't speak in the normal way.

"Yes, you've left your body."

"But how did I change. I mean, last time it was an escape mechanism from..." Shelley gasped for her mind became blank. She felt panicky. Why couldn't she remember?

"Stop it!" Loretta reprimanded. *"If you destabilise yourself it will help nobody. What's wrong and don't tell me nothing. Our communication is more than just words, you know."*

"I can't remember anything."

"I see," Loretta's tone changed to empathy. *"Just relax and look down. Do you recognise yourself?"*

"Yes."

"And the man beside you?"

"My husband, Rhett. No, that's not true. We aren't married yet but will be sometime..." With Loretta's help, memories from when she awoke in the Riversdale sand hills flooded back though

her mind. Everything from going through the portals to meeting Dee and rescuing Corwin, up to Krass with Zarleg and the wagon was remembered. She also knew about and the present situation.

"*And before?*" Loretta asked.

"Before what?"

"*Before you woke up on Earth Alpha and had to steal those clothes.*"

Shelley thought back but drew a blank. Nothing, not even a hazy emotion could be found. "*Nothing,*" she gasped. "*It's as if my life started on that beach.*"

"*You've done better than us,*" Loretta replied.

Shelley was curious and listened intently. According to Loretta, the three identities found they could remember nothing before the funeral service and didn't even know who their dead companions were.

"*When did this start?*" Shelley asked.

"*When the three of us awoke after you had all gone to bed. Irene and Sarine are still trying to find a solution for our amnesia. I came in here and noticed your present form floating above the bed. It took me a while to realise who you were and awaken you.*"

"*Is someone doing this?*"

"*I've no idea. Sarine is the expert in that direction. I think, though that we need to try to deal with our present predicament first.*"

"*How?*"

"*In your identity metamorphous you can fly up the mountain to the top monastery and check to see if the portal is there. Sarine suggests I go with you.*'

"*So somebody made me into an identity so I could do this?*"

"*No,*" replied Sarine. The two other identities had arrived. "*I think your subconscious desire to help activated your ability to leave your body.*"

"*Am I trapped out of my body like you three?*"

"*We don't know,*" Irene said in her Irish brogue. "*Try returning.*"

Shelley felt apprehensive as she approached her body. She touched her skin, jerked and a cold shiver went through her mind. She shook her head and stared out...at the three identities hovering nearby. She glanced down, saw her hand, moved it and realised that, though slightly cold from the missing blankets that had slipped off, she was herself again. She rolled over, hugged Rhett and kissed his cheek.

"*Now come back to us,*" Irene said.

Shelley gulped. She glanced at the ceiling and sort of willed herself to go to it, there was a faint disorientation, not unlike going into a portal and she found herself hovering above her sleeping body.

"I did it!"

"Good," Sarine replied. "So you and Loretta get going. Irene and I will tell Rhett and Krass what happened when they awaken. Take care and if you find the portal, don't enter it. Going though and possibly being trapped in another world will help nobody."

"Come on," Loretta said. *"Just stay close to me and you'll be fine."* She disappeared straight up through the ceiling.

Shelley took one last glance back at Rhett and herself, gulped and followed.

*

CHAPTER EIGHT

The stairs that zigzagged up the mountainside had been newly cut with that raw look of bare earth and rocks. Also the handrails were new. Shelley soon learned, or perhaps remembered, how to move through the air in her identity metamorphosis and her communication with Loretta became as natural as talking and listening. In fact it now seemed as if they were conversing naturally, not just transferring thoughts.

Some aspects of being identities were still scary like when she felt she'd trip on a step. She reached out for the rail for support and found herself flying right through the rail and above a thirty-metre drop over sharp rocks.

"*It's your mind,*" Loretta explained. "*You are so used to using your limbs, you think you still have them. Reaching out to grab a rail is quite natural.*"

"*But finding yourself above a chasm and expecting to fall is somewhat terrifying.*"

"*So come back.*"

Instead Shelley rose up to the next level and waited for Loretta to follow. They continued on until they arrived at the monastery itself. The imposing stonework looked crisp and new. Shelley glanced out at the tower above the cliff. There was a whole new section and the plateau it was built upon was wide with several metres between the new section and where the cliff dropped away. The main entrance was different, too. A deep cut in the rocks stopped any pedestrian from walking up to the walls while the door contained a drawbridge that was raised and held in place by massive chains. On their side of the cutting was a small stone guardhouse.

"*Be careful.*" Loretta said. "*Try to remain in shady areas so you don't reflect back light. It will help if they don't see us.*"

Shelley felt nervous. Two humanoid creatures stood in the guardhouse. They were, though, different from anything Shelley could remember seeing before. They appeared to be males, were two and a half metres tall, slim with shaved faces and heads. There were, though eyebrows and fine hairs on the arms that showed their animal rather than reptilian ancestry. Each wore a long blue gown that extended from a pushed back hood to ankles. A leather belt gathered the gowns around their waists and the only other clothing were simple sandals on otherwise bare feet.

Each guard stood with hiss feet apart and held a round white globe between his folded arms. Both guards stared straight ahead in a formal pose and didn't move.

"*Do you know anything about them?*" Shelley asked.

"Only what I see. They're humans and both males. By the look of this monastery I'd say they are the original inhabitants here. Their clothing suggests they are monks of some religious order, probably with a vow of rising above the basic human needs and wants."

"And the globe in their hands."

"That is a worry. It looks too modern to be a weapon of the era. In a different situation I'd say they were fixed beam emulsifiers or perhaps force field protection devices."

"I don't know about such weapons?"

Loretta's ball vibrated as if she was embarrassed. *"Neither do I, Shelley. The words just came to me. The mist over my memory hasn't lifted."*

*

"Ladies of the Light, your arrival is a month early." The monk on the left spoke in a booming voice while, in the same instance a blue vibrating light radiated from his globe and struck them.

Shelley gasped for she found herself back in her physical body with the only difference being the clothes she wore. It was a silken silver gown that was similar except in colour to the one the monks wore. This was the first time she had seen Loretta except as an unconscious figure but she recognised her at once. She was also dressed in a gown and had sandals on her feet.

The second guard spoke. "Your journey must have been long and arduous, My Ladies. In your physical bodies you may replenish your veins and rest. We shall inform the abbot that you have arrived at our humble abode."

He stared straight at Shelley and she flushed when she realised that, in the daylight the gowns they wore were almost translucent. This was even more embarrassing than her arrival at Riversdale. At least when she was there two men's piercing eyes were not scrutinising her

Loretta though, reacted. "Your eyes are like a man of lust and flesh not one of an holy order," she whispered in a cold voice. "Do not stare at our physical bodies which are but a shell for our inner souls."

The guard's cheeks reddened in embarrassment and he immediately lowered his eyes. "I apologise and will seek immediate penance for my unworthiness, My Lady."

"Three lashes with the knout," the first guard spat. "The punishment will be carried out before evening prayers."

Shelley stared at the pair and realised the second guard was young, a mere youth in fact. He suddenly appeared frightened as he ran a tongue over his dry lips. When he attempted to hide any emotion, his arms shook.

Three lashes for looking at her... this was barbaric!

She reached out and brushed the younger guard's arm. Yes, it was trembling. "Your name?"

"It is forbidden." The youth gazed at his feet.

"Look me in the eyes and tell me your name." She almost added 'please' but decided that that would destroy any authority the guards thought she had.

"He is called Novice 176," the first guard interrupted.

Shelley felt annoyed. She turned and glowered at the first guard. "Who asked you?" she retorted.

The guard hesitated. "Names of the flesh are forbidden here," he said. "We all have assigned numbers."

"And yours?" Loretta asked in her authoritative cold voice.

"Monk 93."

"And you will have Novice 176 whipped for merely gazing at us?"

"To lust for a female body except during the month of repentance is a grave sin deserving such punishment."

"So you will also report for your punishment Monk 93. I believe your eyes were as lustful as those of Novice 176."

"But..."

"You contradict me!" Loretta spat.

The guard paled. "I shall report for my lashings, My Lady."

"No," Shelley cut in. "Neither of us were offended by your worldly thoughts and we forgive you both. There are far more important issues to occupy our minds." She hesitated and hoped she wouldn't overstep any authority she was meant to have. "Neither of you will be punished nor will you speak of this indiscretion again."

Both guards appeared to relax and nodded.

"You agree?" Loretta added.

"Your words are our commands," the older guard said.

"And your real name, Novice 176?" Shelley asked.

The youth caught her eye, switched his gaze to the other guard who gave a slight twist of his lips and answered. "Timothy Bradshaw, My Lady."

Shelley suppressed a gasp of surprise at his English name. Another though rushed into her mind. They were all speaking in English.

"I am Shelley, Timothy and this is Loretta." She felt a slight touch on her hand and caught Loretta's eyes. Oh my stars, she'd done something wrong!

"That is Lady Shelley and Lady Loretta," her friend cut in. "We shall only call you by your given name when we are alone, Timothy." She turned to the older monk. "And your birth name, Monk 93?"

"Peter White, Lady Loretta."

"Thank you Peter. Now all is forgiven and we would like to avail to your hospitality. We are indeed tired after our journey."

Shelley felt Loretta give her hand another tiny squeeze. They would need to be extremely cautious but were committed to entering the monastery. She glanced down at herself and wondered what would happen. Was she really herself or in a duplication of her body lying on the bed in the lower building? Also, could they return to being identities or were they permanently in these bodies. If that was so, how could they get back?

"*I know,*" Loretta's voice entered her mind. "*I am worried, too but we've got to continue. Just maintain a dignity...*"

"*I almost blew it by using our names, didn't I?*" As Shelley thought the words she studied the guards. They did not appear to have 'heard' them.

"*Almost, but I think we have befriended Timothy. Don't trust Peter, though. He is as ruthless as they come.*"

Shelley heard a squeaking sound and turned. The drawbridge was being lowered across the cutting and she could see several more blue-gowned monks waiting in the gateway on the other side.

*

Shelley knew something was wrong as soon as she crossed the bridge. An elderly man in a purple gown surrounded by four monks in dark-blue gowns stood at the end of a double row. Twenty or more monks dressed like Timothy and Peter lined up on either side of a pathway.

"I am Abbot One and have already communicated with our god about you both." The man in the purple gown stared at Shelley as the line of monks closed in behind Loretta and herself. A leer crossed his face sent a cold shiver through her spine. "You are early and corrupt our souls."

"Perhaps the moon is inconsistent, Abbot," one of the deep blue clad monks said. "They may have been sent to serve."

The abbot turned. "Your thoughts are lustful, High Priest 6. You set a bad example."

"Think of the morale if the time is brought forward, Abbot." The priest gave a head bow,

Shelley turned, saw a white faced Loretta and realised they were in deep trouble. Hands grabbed her from behind and she was held in a vice grip. Even worse, though were wandering fingers that reached through and squeezed her breast. She gasped but became determined not to scream. Another hand covered her mouth and a voice whispered in her ear.

"You will stand still and respect Abbot One." It was Peter who was holding her.

"May I speak, My Lord?" A nervous Timothy stepped forward.

The abbot glanced up. "What is it Novice...err." He glanced at a number sewn on Timothy's collar "176"

"Shouldn't our goddess be consulted about the new arrivals?"

Abbot One glowered and Timothy appeared terrified. "Chapter 6, Section 78, Line 7 of the Scribes states any request about communication with our goddess can be asked without fear of retribution, My Lord."

"Fool," cried High Priest 6. "Why would a goddess be interested in a lowly Novice?"

'I was a guard on duty...'' Timothy muttered.

"He has a point 6," Abbot One whispered. "What do you suggest 176?"

"Seek advice in our afternoon prayers, My Lord. Our goddess may be able to advise us why these Ladies of Light arrived."

"The boy's a fool who should be flogged," High Priest 6 grunted.

"But he made an interesting comment. Who are we to disobey the advice from a goddess of a realm from whence they may have come?" He turned, stared at Shelley and purposely dropped his eyes to her heaving breasts. "We shall do as the young man suggests and unless our goddess intervenes, he will be allowed to experience the pleasures of the flesh with the body you stole." He stepped forward and squeezed Shelley's cheeks. "On second thought, your companion can service him. Someone of your beauty shouldn't be wasted on a novice." He chuckled. "The goddess of fertility may even offer her blessing to our union."

"Bastard," Shelley hissed.

"Possibly, I am. This world is filled with evil." The abbot smirked and turned to the monks. "Take the women to the dungeon, feed them and give them amenities to bathe and care for their bodies. They shall, however, not be touched until after we have spoken to our goddess."

Shelley turned her head to see Timothy standing beside her. "Thank you," she whispered. "You gave us time."

"Not enough, I'm afraid," the youth replied. "The prayers finish at six." He reached forward and touched her arm. "I'm sorry but I can do no more." He turned and stepped back as Shelley and Loretta were frogmarched away.

*

Shelley's resistance collapsed when she was literally thrown in a dank cell. She landed on her knees and elbows. For a moment she kneeled on the stone floor as emotions exploded and she burst into shuddering tears. It helped and when the tears became sniffs she managed to look around and take stock. Skin was ripped off her knees and one elbow with blood oozing from scratches. Both arms were bruised from fingerprints and her gown was tucked up above her knees. She grabbed a nearby board for support and staggered to her feet.

A pale light from an outside oil lamp flickered to show her surroundings, not that there was much. The cell had bunks on one side with a thin mattress on the bottom one and wooden slates on the upper. The walls were made of stones covered in grime and one corner, green slime. The only other item in the room was a tin bucket in the corner, her toilet apparently.

She turned to the door. This was solid except for a twenty-centimetre square in the middle made secure by two vertical iron bars. She could smell oil smoke and saw a flaming torch attached to the opposite wall. As far as she could see corridor was empty,

"Loretta," she called in a hushed voice. "Can you hear me?"

"Of course." Her friend's voice came from behind. Shelley swung around. An identity hovered above the bunk. *"I'm in the adjacent cell. How are you?"*

"Scared."

"They don't act like pious monks, do they?"

"I don't know," Shelley whispered. "In my world only the elderly followed religions..."

"...And you remember?"

"Not really. I ...oh hell..." Shelley looked down at herself, collapsed on the cell floor. She was an identity again. *"So we fly out and go home?"*

"It's not that easy, I'm afraid. Our bodies are still trapped here."

"But we won't be much use to the monks if we are unconscious."

"Remember the ball. I'm sure that when it is fired we will find ourselves back in our bodies and subject to attack."

"But we can fly out and tell Rhett or Krass."

"I tried but a force field surrounds the monastery. This place is more than it seems. You were out cold for an hour. I came back to check on you."

"So what do we do?"

"I unsuccessfully tried to contact Sarine and Irene but my telepathy was blocked. I think it is the same force field that keeps us here. You may be able to get through, though."

"How?"

"Telepathy is stronger between people who are genetically related."

"Rhett?"

"No, he is not related to you. I was thinking of your children. It has also been proved that they are easier to contact. It's like the ability of young children to learn a second language easily. Try it, and then we'll explore this monastery. We have a couple of hours before those prayers are over. This dungeon is locked but there are no guards down here so our bodies should be safe for now."

Shelley frowned and turned her thoughts into trying to communicate with her children. She got through to Dee but the signal faded and she lost contact, just as if someone had hung up an old fashioned telephone.

"It sounded promising," Loretta praised. *"Try reaching Corwin. The younger a child is, the easier it is for them to receive telepathy"*

*

"Daddy," Dee screamed. "Where's Mum?"

Rhett saw his daughter's look of anxiety and felt a quiver in his own stomach. After he had awoken and found Shelley's side of the bed empty he had assumed she had gone for an early morning stroll. An hour had passed since then and he had just begun to worry himself.

Irene's voice filled his mind. *"You'd better come through, Rhett. There's a development..."*

Rhett grabbed Dee's hand and tore though to the laboratory where the identities' bodies lay. He moved up to Krass and gazed over his shoulder. There were only two women lying on the slabs... Loretta had gone!

"Where are they?" Rhett's worry deepened.

"They went up to the top monastery together," Krass muttered.

"Together! How?"

"Shelley became a identity like us," Sarine hovered in front of Rhett. *"She left her body in sound condition next to you."*

"But the bed's empty!" Rhett screamed. "They've both gone... disappeared into thin air." He grabbed Krass's arm in a, none too light hold. "Why did you let them go?"

"He didn't. If it was anyone who allowed it, blame me." Sarine said.

Rhett let Krass go. "Sorry," he muttered. "I know you wouldn't do anything to harm Shelley."

"It's all right, Lad," the old man said. "We are as worried as you. More happened..." In a soft voice, Krass told about the memory losses and about Shelley being able to return to her body. "We think that she needed to return to her physical body up there and is in it right now."

Rhett stared at the old man. "But that doesn't explain Loretta. She can't return to her body."

"But that must be exactly what happened," Irene said.

"So go and get them!" Corwin stood across the room with his sister's arms around him.

'There's an army out there surrounding us," Rhett replied. "How can we get through?"

"We could go," Sarine said.

Krass held up his hand. "No. What if something also happened to you both and your bodies just vanished? Perhaps Shelley and Loretta are safe and will return in a few hours,"

Rhett began to feel desperate.

"They may return as identities and their bodies reappear?" Irene said.

Rhett frowned. Wasn't that how Shelley arrived at Riversdale in the first place? This was possible. "So we wait?" he asked.

"No," Dee screamed. "We can't. Something has happened to Mum and Loretta. I know..." She burst into tears. "I don't know how I know but deep down inside me, I heard Mum calling for help!'

Corwin's lips trembled. "I did too. Mum told me to stay away from the front of the tower. There are evil guards and a drawbridge."

Rhett squatted down and took Corwin's hands. "And Mum told you that?"

The little boy nodded. "She's locked up in a dungeon and is scared, Daddy. The human men there are going to fight her and Loretta."

"He means rape..." Dee howled as more tears rolled down her cheeks.

*

CHAPTER NINE

Their plan to get through the surrounding girifa warriors was crude but the best they could decide upon at such short notice. The humans, including the children who couldn't be left behind, sat in the wagon that had been reinforced with wooden slates placed beneath the canvas and across the back. The two identities said they would provided an escort by circling around the wagon and, hopefully, frightening the superstitious warriors away.

"Ready?" Krass called from where he stood beside the chain that cranked the main gate up.

Rhett glanced back at the children huddled in the wagon and signalled that he was ready while Zarleg sat like a monstrous runner on a starting block.

When Krass cranked the chain wheel, the gate rose, the identities disappeared from sight through and gap and Zarleg let out a roar that even surprised Rhett. After the gate was raised high enough, Zarleg moved forward, so quickly that the front wagon wheels rose off the ground. Luckily, the rear ones gripped the cobblestones and the creaking, swaying vehicle almost sideswiped the archway as he galloped through.

He continued to roar but stopped and waited for a moment. Krass released a holding brake on the chain wheel and charged through the gap, mere seconds before the gate crashed down. He reached the wagon and clamoured in the back.

"Go, Dad!" Dee screamed.

Zarleg charged ahead. Rhett held the reins and concentrated on keeping the wagon wheels facing the front as they bounced around, spinning in the air as often as they hit the turf below. He could see little beyond the tsintaosaurus's back and used his feet to steady himself. Corwin crawled up beside him and peeped through a gap in the wood.

"It's working," he cried. "Sarine and Irene are scaring the warriors away." He laughed in nervous excitement. "They're running, Daddy. They're running away."

"Good!" Rhett replied. He wouldn't let go the reins for he was afraid the wagon could tip.

Something banged and Dee screamed.

"It's okay," Krass shouted from behind. "An arrow has just come through the wood. No damage, though."

For ten minutes, Zarleg galloped forward but Rhett was worried. He remembered Krass telling him that the tsintaosaurus could only maintain a high speed for a short time. When he tired the girifa would be over the element of confusion and probably attack. The track ahead ran towards the hills and Rhett recognised the top monastery in the distance with an extra tower on the cliff side. A hand gripped his shoulder.

"We did it, Rhett," the old man said. "The girifa warriors are not chasing us."

"But could be waiting ahead?"

"No. That's not their style. They recognise our bravery and will leave us now."

Krass sat beside Rhett, took the reins and called for Zarleg to slow. The swaying wagon became less of a shaking death trap and the children smiled, though their white faces and clenched fists clinging to the framework showed their anxiety.

Rhett moved a slab of wood aside so he had room and leaned out to survey their surroundings. The lower monastery and the girifa were out of sight. The grassland looked silent and almost friendly with a blue sky above them. They continued on for several more moments before Krass called a halt.

The two identities flew in and hovered beside the wagon.

"The steps up to the monastery are just ahead," Irene said. *"However, there is a guard house at the top manned by two guards."*

"I would advise against going up the steps," Sarine cautioned. *"There is no cover and we'll be seen before we get half way up."* Her tiny ball shape quivered. *"There is some sort of force field surrounding the area so we may not be able to accompany you all the way."*

"So what do we do?" Rhett felt that queasy feeling of hopelessness.

"There is a back route," Sarine said. *"It is a windy zigzag track that is overgrown and looks unused. It was probably the original access when the monastery was being built."*

"There's more," Irene added with excitement in her voice. *"This track stops a hundred metres below the back wall."*

Rhett frowned. "Isn't that bad?"

The identity glowed. *"While Sarine stayed back in case something happened, I had a closer look. There's a tunnel that goes into the cliff."*

"That's logical," Krass said. "Most of these monasteries have back entrances."

"In case there was a siege like the one around us?" Dee asked.

Krass smiled. "Nothing so exciting, Dee. They are used to take in food and other supplies. I wouldn't be surprised if the tunnel leads up through the dungeons to the kitchen."

"That's where Mummy is," Corwin whispered.

"Possibly," Krass said. "But don't build your hopes too high, Lad. Often there's a rabbit warren of tunnels and rooms beneath these buildings. We could be within a wall's width of your mum and not even know."

"We'll know," Corwin said confidently.

"How close can we get with the wagon?" Rhett asked.

"There's no proper track but if we go to the left around the base of the hill it's about a kilometre," Sarine said.

*

It happened so suddenly that Rhett froze. They were on a rise behind a clump of trees when he heard screams. Something hit the wagon roof with a thump and there was a second distinct thump behind the wagon. He glanced at the others, swung down to the ground and ran around the back to look.

On the ground lay two women, one the Asian girl and the other a redhead with pale skin. Both were dressed in silver gowns. They sat up looking bruised and a flabbergasted.

"It just happened without warning," Irene gasped for the redhead was obviously herself. "I was flying above the wagon when I crashed to the ground." She stood up and brushed herself down. "I'm human again but with these ridiculous clothes."

Sarine frowned. "I think we inadvertently went through a force field."

"But you're okay?" Rhett said.

"If you call falling four metres and bouncing off the wagon okay." Irene mumbled.

"It broke your fall," Sarine laughed. "I only fell a metre."

Rhett grinned and helped the pair to their feet behind the now stationary wagon. The others came around and stared at the trio.

"Oh my stars," Krass muttered. "Sarine and Irene?"

"In the flesh," Irene said. "And damned cold in this flimsy gown."

"I'll get you some of Mum's clothes." Dee disappeared into the wagon and returned a moment later with a bundle of clothing in her arms while Krass walked cautiously back though the grass where the wagon had been.

He returned with a frown and asked Rhett to have a look. About fifteen metres back, there was a gap in the trees with a clear view of the monastery above them. He could see the white walls, a cutting with a drawbridge lowered across it. There was also a small guard outhouse on the steps side of the cutting.

"Get down!" Krass screamed.

Rhett dived sideways into a clump of grass just as a blue ray cut across above him.

"Someone fired at us from the guardhouse," Krass gasped.

"With the weapon that hit the identities and made them revert to their bodies," Krass replied.

Both men lay down and peeped through the grass at the guardhouse.

"There goes our element of surprise," Rhett muttered.

"I'd say so," Krass muttered. "That's more than just a monastery of monks up there. I think we'll need help."

"But from where?"

Krass scowled. "I'll speak to Zarleg."

They both retreated to the wagon and Rhett watched as the old man walked up to the tsintaosaurus who bent his head down and appeared to be listening. The old man gestured and spoke in a soft conversation that Rhett couldn't hear while Zarleg grunted and blinked at the appropriate times. Finally he gave a low grumble and raised his head high.

Krass came across. "You want brute force?" he asked.

"As long as Shelley and Loretta aren't caught in the middle of it. What do you have in mind?"

Krass stroked his beard and turned to Dee who had joined them under the trees where they could see the monastery but remain hidden. "What was monastery was like when you first arrived here and met your Mum and Dad?" he asked.

Dee stared out at the distant building. "There was no guardhouse, drawbridge or cutting. I just walked in through the gateway." She pointed up. "There's also an extra tower now."

"That's right," Rhett said. "The portal we came through opened out into a crumbled ruins. The tower must have fallen down the cliff. Erosion over the years, I guess."

Krass nodded and turned to the children. "How do you feel?" he asked.

"Worried about Mum but okay," Dee whispered.

"No dizziness or feeling of not being here?"

"No."

"And you Corwin?"

"My stomach feels funny but I think I'm okay."

Krass walked across and hugged both children. "Aye, you're both fine so your Mum will be okay."

"You mean that if Shelley got killed the children wouldn't be here?" Rhett asked.

Krass nodded. "You know more about this space time stuff than me but isn't it logical?"

"So what is about to happen would have already happened in Rhett's family's time?" Irene asked.

"If the correct scenario is played out," warned Sarine. "Nothing is certain."

The old man stroked his beard and appeared to be deep in thought. "I don't know about you lot but I'm hungry. Let's find a sheltered spot out of range from that guardhouse and rest up. "

*

Shelley glanced down at her body lying below her and turned to Loretta hovering in identity form beside her.

"I think I got through to Corwin," she said. *"He was listening, I know but didn't seem to know how to reply."*

"Can he still hear you?"

Shelley frowned. *"No, I don't think so. Perhaps I can only get through when he's asleep."*

"Okay. Keep trying but now you're with me, I want to explore this monastery further."

There were no other prisoners in the cells but through the end barred door, stairs led down to a lower dungeon as well as upwards. The lower stairwell was dark and appeared unused with dust and spider webs everywhere.

"We'll go up," Loretta said.

Shelley floated behind her companion up to an area that looked like the monks' dormitory. There was a long corridor with open-sided cells on each side. Each contained a narrow bed, end table on which a book was placed and a robe hanging from a hook. Blankets were folded neatly at the end of a small mattress. There were no pillows or other personal items. Unlike the cells they had been locked in, there was a tiny window at the end of each cell with a view of the valley below.

It was so austere that Shelley shuddered.

The end room was an ablutions block consisting of a community shower with a couple of dozen shower heads and pulleys with ropes hanging from the rafters, each holding a towel tied in a knot.

"They wrap their clothes with their towel and pull it above the showers before the water is turned on," Loretta said. *"I don't think individuality is encouraged."*

"It's awful," Shelley replied when she saw the toilets, a row of two boards with a gap between them, a channel beneath and a pipe disappearing through an end wall. She had to admit, though that the place was spotlessly clean with a smell of disinfectant in the air.

They flew on into a deserted courtyard and across to an opened double door. Shelley couldn't resist a gasp as she studied at the scene before her. Inside, the monks all sat crouched on a marble floor with their heads bowled. At the front, with a ray of afternoon sunlight shining on it, was a gigantic stone statue of a standing woman. She was nude but hair consisting of snakes hung down to cover her breasts and crotch. She held two babies, one of each gender, in her arms and stared ahead through black diamond eyes. Suspended half a metre above the snakes was a crown of seven sided stars and different sized golden circles.

"Goddess Arianrhod, keeper of the stars and time, symbol of beauty, fertility and reincarnation," Loretta said. *"I think that is why we were thrown in the dungeon."*

"They think we're her?"

"No. I remember studying ancient religions at university. As I

understand it, the monks are not allowed to have worldly goods or desires, hence their living quarters. However, for one moon cycle a year, they are allowed to taste the sins of the flesh to appease the goddess. Women are provided and the monks mate with them for this month of sin or until every female is impregnated. Usually twenty or more women from nunneries or villages are brought in for the month."

"But according to Krass there are no human women here."

"True but do the monks know that?"

"And we are the first women they've seen?" Shelley gasped.

"Probably, but it is the wrong month. That's why Timothy's suggestion of consulting the goddess was agreed to. No doubt that is what is happening now."

Shelley paled. "And afterwards?"

"We'll either be raped by every monk here until we are impregnated or declared heretics."

"Meaning?"

"We'll be locked in a chamber of with poisonous snakes. The snakes' bite is fatal."

Shelley felt ill. "Pleasant religion."

The prayer ended, the monks moved to sit cross-legged on the floor and a dark-blue gowned monk stood up. He faced the statue and spoke loud angry words in an unknown language.

"The ancient druid language," Loretta said. "Come on, let's go."

*

They flew back out and along to another stairway. Upstairs was a factory floor with one massive room supported by stone poles and divided into sections. One section contained quite exquisite furniture in various stages of construction; another had a firing chamber and pottery of all sizes and shapes. The finished products were brightly coloured and covered in beautiful scenes. A third area was a clothing factory with trundle sewing machines. Ordinary vintage clothes, as well as monks' robes hung from racks suspended from the roof. Yet another area was for artists with mainly landscape paintings of animals, birds and trees stacked along a wall or placed on large easels.

"It's wrong," Shelley said.

"What is?" asked Loretta.

"The paintings and the pottery show animals and birds but Krass told us this world only has reptilian creatures like Zarleg." She pointed to a painting of a farmyard. "There are no horses and cows here like in that scene"

"That's right."

"So the monks are not from this world." Shelley felt excited. "Therefore, they must have arrived from another world. The portal must be here."

"We only came up two floors. There must be at least another eight in the towers. Let's go on and look."

The floor above was deserted and a complete contrast to the clean floors below. Rubbish dirt, dust and cobwebs were everywhere. Even the light was dim because the windows were covered in grime. They flew on and made another discovery. The only stairwells led back down to the factory floor. There were none that led up to the towers above.

"But more floors are there," Shelley murmured. *"When Dee found us, we went down stairs from the ruined tower. It's there, too. We saw it from the valley when we arrived."*

"So we fly through the ceiling and look," Loretta said. *"Being an identity does have some advantages,"*

*

"Oh no." Shelley gasped as they came up though the floor into an ultramodern metallic room.

This wasn't a monastery but a modern life support base with military personnel sitting or walking silently around a massive control room. An officer dressed in a black commander's uniform with a swastika on the sleeve turned.

She immediately recognised him. It was Abbot One!

*

CHAPTER TEN

Rhett wanted the children to remain with Krass and Zarleg at the wagon while he investigated the tunnel. However, Dee stared at him with a stubborn expression on her face and refused to stay.

"Mum may need me," she stated. "My earrings are giving a loud beeping noise so I know she's close."

"And I'm the only one she talks to in my head," Corwin added to the argument.

"They're both right," Krass added. "I will stay here with Zarleg." He turned to the two women. "If we split up, Rhett will need another adult with him."

Irene glanced at Sarine. "I'll go."

"We'll give you an hour," Sarine replied. "If you have problems, don't try anything dangerous. Get back to us."

Rhett nodded. "I won't risk anything while I have the children." He smiled and placed a few supplies in his backpack, tested his torch and glanced at Irene. "Will you take up the rear?"

"Sure."

He held out the end of a small rope he'd wrapped around his waist to the children. "You two hold the rope and stick close. If either of you get any messages or different noises in your minds or ears, tell us immediately, no matter how unimportant it seems."

Dee and Corwin both nodded. Irene did their jacket buttons up and went up to Zarleg. She rubbed his neck and gave both Krass and Sarine a hug before nodding to Rhett that she was ready to go.

*

The obviously artificial tunnel had smooth brick walls that curved in above them just a few centimetres higher than Rhett's head. Every twenty metres or so there were brass holders fastened to the wall with the remains of candles covered in melted wax. Everything was covered by thick layers of dust and cobwebs. The air had a slightly musty odour but a slight breeze in his face indicated that there was another exit.

They walked in silence with only their footsteps echoing on the stone floor. The entrance behind disappeared in the distance until only light from Rhett and Irene's torches show the way.

Rhett stopped five minutes later and turned to the children. "Any change?" he asked.

"The buzz in my ear tells me we are going the right way," Dee whispered. In the eerie conditions even her hushed voice produced an echo.

"I hear poetry," Corwin appeared nervous. "A man is saying poetry. It's very faint but is getting louder."

Dee turned to her brother and grabbed his arm. She clapped her hand to her left earring and listened with a frown on her face. "I hear it, too. It's not poetry, Corwin but a man..." She turned to Rhett. "You know, what people do in a church."

"You mean praying?" Rhett asked.

"That's it. The man is praying for his goddess to help him get free."

"Goddess not god?" Irene asked.

"Yes, he asked if 'she' could help, not 'he'." Dee held her hand up and squeezed Corwin's arm tighter as she listened.

"He called her Goddess Arrowhead," Corwin almost shouted.

"Head...head...head," his voice echoed

"Could that be Arianrhod?" Irene asked.

Corwin flushed. "That's it?'

"And who's she?" Rhett asked.

"Early humans had gods and goddesses to represent everything in her lives. I think she was something to do with life or death... no that's not right... it was birth and fertility. Many monasteries were built to worship just one god or goddess. This one could have been built to worship her."

"How stupid!" Dee retorted.

"To us, possibly," Irene replied. "But we should never berate others because they think differently than we do. Didn't they teach you that at school?"

"I guess," Dee whispered.

"The man's frightened," Corwin continued. "But not just for himself."

"Who for then?" Rhett asked.

"The monks. He's afraid the monastery monks will be hurt by evil."

"Evil what?"

"Humans that came through the portal."

"Are you sure?" Rhett gasped.

"He's right Dad," Dee said. "He said that these humans are more evil than the worse girifa and has asked his goddess to destroy them."

"Perhaps that's our job." Irene's were eyes wide in the torchlight.

They lapsed into silence as they moved slowly forward.

Dee grabbed Rhett's sleeve. "We've gone too far," she gasped.

"Your beeps tell you?"

Dee nodded. "Just now." She let go the rope, squeezed past Irene and walked back half a dozen steps. Her face screwed up in concentration as she spun around, faced to her left, before turning to face the opposite direction. "Here!"

Rhett examined the wall. It appeared no different from anywhere else with the brickwork almost seamless as it sloped up to the ceiling above. There were no cracks or broken pieces, whatsoever. However, when he ran his hand over an area about waist height one brick felt soft like jelly. It consisted of a putty-like substance that he could squeeze with his fingers.

While the others watched, he pulled a glob out, handed it to Irene and reached further into the gap. More and more pieces came out until he had created a cavity the size of half a brick.

"It goes in further but the soft part is getting smaller," he whispered.

"Let me," Dee said. "My hands are smaller than yours."

Rhett withdrew his hand and watched as Dee reached in and brought out small amounts of the putty. Finally she stopped. "There's a handle," she said. "It's metal. What shall I do?"

"Let me see." Rhett squatted down and shone his torch into the hole. It looked like an inverted cone with a brass handle about a hand's length in. He reached forward but his fingers were too large to do more than touch it. "I think it might turn. Can you try, Dee?"

Dee nodded, placed her tongue between her lips in concentration, and reached in. She frowned in concentration as he fingers twisted. "It's coming!"

With a creak, a section of the wall ahead pivoted inwards. Light poured in through a crack that widened to reveal a flaming lamp.

"By the forgiveness of Goddess Arianrhod, who are you?" a timid male voice spoke out.

As the stuffy smell of sweat and dampness hit his nose, Rhett reached forward and pushed the door open. He was in a corridor directly opposite a row of cell doors. Behind one barred door, an elderly man with a white beard and gaunt features gripped the bars. He looked unkempt in a dirty and ripped purple gown. But his eyes were alive.

"Children!" the man gasped. "A family! The goddess has replied to my prayers. Welcome my family from Arianrhod. I am Abbot One who, until imprisoned in this dungeon by the evil ones, was the spiritual leader of this monastery." He smiled. "But call me Victor, my given name."

*

"They're from the parallel universe," Loretta said. *"I'd say they're speaking in Earth 7 so I can't understand a word they're saying."*

Loretta's identity ball showed as a low dim as if she was completely puzzled. Shelley's own sensation was weird. The words that she heard and the ideas in her mind were different yet she could understand what the man she knew as Abbot One was saying. Of course, the language, Earth 7 was one of the interworld's thirty-seven official languages, ten of which came from Earth Alpha. She didn't know how she knew this but just did. The language being spoken was German which was unknown to her. However, the words in her mind were translated into English.

"*I may know why,*" Loretta said after Shelley explained the situation. "*You hear German but your earrings translates the language into English. That's why I can't understand it. Listen carefully. That abbot seems frustrated about something. Fly closer so we can hear his conversation but stay in the shadows.*"

Loretta thought back but no other memories came to the fore. She floated towards the ceiling, hugged a far wall and moved across until she came to a recess between two vertical cabinets. Unless someone looked directly in the gap she would be invisible to those below.

"What do you mean, you lost it?" Abbot One's voice wasn't raised but the tone portrayed a ruthless authority that made Shelley shiver.

A man dressed in a white technician's coat glanced up from the semi-transparent sphere that his hands were inside. Shelley could see his fingers moving as if they were using a keyboard. At the same time, line after line of mathematical symbols appeared on a screen ahead of him. "The signals are being interfered with and destabilized, Commander Jung."

"By whom?" Jung, the name must be Abbot One's real one, did raise his voice. "Six weeks on this primitive planet and everything was perfect. We even brought supplies in through the portal and now, you say it's stopped working. Explain that, Doctor Fuchs."

"It's still working, Commander but cannot be controlled. Something is breaking down the quantum physics interchange." The scientist pointed to the screen. "Instead of a stable point of entry it diverges on a random path. If we entered the portal now we could end up anywhere."

"Another portal?"

"Oh yes. You must have two portals to complete a circuit. It's like electricity with a loose wire. No connection, no current."

"I know that" Jung grunted. "You told me everything was ready. All we had to do was to expand the size so we can bring in the aircraft."

"That's true. This new signal isn't from the portal itself, though. It is a local signal being broadcast from within a kilometre radius."

"Here! The girifa are primitive. They don't even know there are other worlds; let alone how to travel between them. The human monks in this monastery aren't much better."

Fuchs nodded. "I believe the women we caught came in through the portal but not from our universe."

"Go on."

"Once here, they set up a transmitter to cut us off from home. Data shows they are similar humans to us with no genetic deviation. My theory is that they're from our future and have travelled back to this time to stop us expanding our empire."

"But our future keeps going. We know that."

"It did, Commander." Fuchs wriggled his fingers and a three dimensional diagram appeared in front of the screen above him. 'This is a computer simulation a thousand times simplified but the yellow and red lines ..." His voice continued.

Shelley had seen something like this before. It showed two alternatives, the yellow line continued but the red one burst into a hundred sparks that almost immediately faded.

"Our universe is the red line. Unless we can stop it, we will have no future. Instead that yellow one will be the only significant one that continues on through space-time."

"And how is this one different?"

"In that universe the Americans discovered the atomic bomb, not us. They used it first in 1945 to win that war."

"And the great German people were destroyed."

Fuchs flushed. "Not really," he muttered. "Our country was divided into two ideologies for fifty years but later became a mid-sized democratic country."

"Ruled by Jews?" Jung could barely hide his anger

"This is only a computer prediction, Commander. However, the probability that our life as we know it will be destroyed is over ninety-six percent certain. This ties in with my theory that the women we captured are responsible for everything that is happening."

Jung stood and turned. "I knew we should have killed them straight away. Get the guards down there and destroy them."

"We'll blow our cover with the monks."

"So? They've outlived their usefulness anyway.'

Shelley hastily repeated the gist of the conversation to Loretta.

'*We need to get back,*" her friend hissed.

"*But how can we help ourselves down there?*"

"*I have no idea,*" Loretta retorted. "*I do know that if our bodies are destroyed we'll die. Our only chance is to escape from our cells in our physical bodies before the guards arrive.*"

*

Rhett listened intently to the old man who said he was the real abbot. Apparently, the monastery had been invaded by ruthless humans who came through a 'magic' door, that could only be a portal. The top hierarchy of the order were captured and a new clandestine order established in its place.

"And the monks accepted them?" Rhett asked.

"It happens. Often the leaders in a monastery are shifted onto other sectors and a new team arrives. The ordinary monks and novices are expected to obey and not question the authority as it is the will of the goddess for this to happen."

"So how many are real monks?" Irene asked.

Victor sighed. "Ten of us were replaced. They've all gone except me."

"Where?' Irene asked.

"Through the door the ruthless ones arrived from. Whether it is the realm of the dead or those awaiting to be born, I do not know."

Rhett studied the abbot. He was obviously from a primitive society and believed in the goddess he served. "But why are you still here in this dungeon cell?" he asked.

"They need my skills and knowledge to control the monks."

"And you help them?" Irene retorted.

"I have told them about procedures and customs. Inner secrets remain hidden from them all."

"What secrets?" Irene asked.

"My young maiden with the hair of fire, it would not be a secret it was divulged, now would it?"

Irene flushed. "I'm sorry," she muttered.

"But we can help each other," Rhett said.

"Dad," Dee tugged on Rhett's sleeve. "Stop gossiping! We need to find Mum. Time's running out."

Rhett turned. "You got a message from her."

"Only an emotion."

"She's heading for trouble." Corwin sounded anxious. "It may already be too late."

Victor turned to the boy. "Voices of the angels come to you, My Son?"

Corwin shrugged. "Something like that," he muttered.

The abbot turned to Rhett. "Keys to the cells are hanging on that yonder nail. If you let me out I can guide you through this building. Hidden stairs and passageways abound. Even I don't know them all but the ones I do know of can take us through the upper floors away from even their electronic surveillance monitors."

Irene looked surprised "You know of these?"

Victor raised his eyebrows. "The ways of religion and science are blurred. I know that these things are human or girifa made though it helps to ignore the fact for the sake of believers."

Rhett grinned slightly as he looked for the keys. Perhaps he was wrong about the old fellow. The abbot was remarkably astute and knew more than admitted. He found the keys and unlocked the cell door. When he helped Victor up he noted how thin and undernourished he was.

"They told me that if I needed to have food, I had to exchange information," Victor whispered. "Luckily they think I'm a fool and believe the blasphemous half-truths I feed them. Deep down, they are afraid of me and that is why I am still alive." He walked out and turned towards a narrow corridor that was almost hidden in the gloom between two empty cells. "This way. If your friends are in this monastery we'll find them."

*

"They're here!" Jung screamed. "Shoot to kill."

Shelley followed Loretta down towards the floor. Just before the stone floor surrounded her, a beam shot from across the room and she felt a buzzing sensation. She could see the unused room below but something was wrong! Pain ripped through her body, she felt herself falling and saw her body, arms and legs spread out. Oh my stars, she had returned to her physical body. Her downward drop stopped as pain so sever, she couldn't stop a cry of anguish, throbbed from her right leg. She swung around in a circle and found herself dangling, upside down from the ceiling. Her leg and foot were being crushed. In those few seconds it took her to realise what had happened, the pressure increased. It was as if solid rock was squashing it.

"Wriggle your foot," Loretta screamed from above her.

No, she was beneath her gazing up from where she had landed in a heap on the floor. Shelley strained, arched her back and flung her hands out. She managed to grip something, bite on her lip to try to ignore the throbbing pain in her right leg as blotches of purple passed through her mind.

Loretta stood up, grabbed her shoulders and lifted. With the weight removed from her one stuck leg, the pain was relieved a fraction and Shelley was able to work out what had happened.

"Wriggle your foot," Loretta repeated. "It got stuck in the stonework between the floors when we metamorphosed back into our physical bodies. The longer you wait the worse it will become."

Shelley understood and with an unsuppressed shriek, managed to ignore the pain and turn her foot.

"Almost," Loretta gasped as she continued to support her. "I see cracks appearing around it."

Shelley gritted her teeth, took a deep breath and attempted to move her foot once again. It felt as if some giant had seized her and was trying to break every bone there. Hot spasms of agony shot up her leg and through her lower body. She managed to place her free foot against the ceiling and use it to push.

"I can't!" she screamed almost hysterically as perspiration dripped into her eyes. She persevered though, there was a crack like a whip and she fell straight down on top of Loretta. They were both pelted by a shower of dust and rubble but she was free!

*

Rhett stared at Irene and Victor as a distinct crash echoed through the walls of the upper dungeon. Everything was happening and it wasn't all good. They'd found Shelley and Loretta in adjacent cells but both women were unconscious and there were no handy keys available to unlock the doors. He was looking for something to force the cell doors open when Dee's cold trembling hand grabbed his

"Look!" she gasped.

Both the sleeping women began to become transparent when, first their limbs and later their bodies and faces became ghostlike with the bunks they were lying on showing through them. Within a minute, all that could be seen was a blurred silhouetted outline of their bodies. Loretta disappeared first but Shelley seemed to change from the middle outwards with her legs and face remaining solid while the rest of her body faded. Her lips moved and for a second her eyes appeared to open. They looked terrified and her mouth contorted into a silent scream.

"Mummy's caught in the wall!" Corwin shouted. "Do something!"

Rhett grabbed the little boy and hugged him close as he stared at Shelley's face, which faded from sight. All that remained was one leg from the calf muscle down to the ankle, foot and toes. But more was happening! The foot became squeezed and misshapen, two elongated scratches appeared and blood oozed out. The foot wriggled and turned, moved slightly and more blood flowed out.

"What's happening?" Rhett cried.

"If an identity changes back while inside a solid object it is squashed. I think she got her foot stuck in a wall that she flew through." Irene replied.

Rhett felt both children's trembling hands in his as he stared at the foot. It moved again and gradually began to fade.

"She's getting it out," Irene whispered. "And not a moment too soon. If the pressure became too great she would have lost the leg and possibly bled to death."

The leg faded until it, along with the surrounding blood vanished.

"So where are they?" Rhett gasped.

"Upstairs," Verton whispered. "Come on. There is another back stairwell we can use that goes right up the back tower. It will be the best way to go"

"Why?" Rhett asked.

"It is the oldest tower in the monastery and is unused. I think the enemy have converted it for their own uses." He grimaced. "It began before they made their presence known and kidnapped my priests and myself. My monks were too afraid to investigate and unfortunately I never forced anyone to check."

"Mummy's still in trouble." Corwin burst into sobbing howls that not even Rhett or Dee could pacify. "If the men aren't stopped they will get to her first."

CHAPTER ELEVEN

Sarine was regretting that she had agreed to stay with Krass and the wagon for nothing had happened and there had been no communication with the others. That was the disadvantage of being in your physical body. As identities she could be over a kilometre from the others and still be in touch. She watched as Krass dragged a sack of oats from the wagon, cut the top open and held it out for Zarleg.

"This is the last one, old fellow," he said. "If you gobble it all at once, you'll go hungry tomorrow." He frowned when the tsintaosaurus ignored the food and stared in the tunnel mouth. He listened to the creature grunt and nodded. "They're in trouble and need help, you say? What sort of trouble? "

Sarine glanced at him. "This is not the time to be fantasising, Krass," she said. "We need to do something soon. They've been away too long."

Krass turned to her. "Zarleg told me that we need to destroy the tower closest to the cliff. It is filled with evil ones with modern stuff that will destroy not only our friends but everyone else too."

"Stuff?"

Krass shrugged. "Zarleg's explanation."

"And you talk to him?"

"Half talk. He has a rudimentary language but conveys his thoughts mainly through images of the mind. I guess it's like your communication as an identity."

Sarine nodded and turned to Zarleg. "So why don't you talk to me, too?" she asked.

Immediately emotions filled her mind. She felt frightened and defenceless. Zarleg's yellow eyes turned to her and he grunted. "*It is difficult to communicate with humans but I will try. The emotion you feel is from Corwin. He is terrified and ...*"

Sarine was used to telepathy but the message she received was not only through Corwin's eyes but also filtered by Zarleg's interpretation of the world around him. Krass squeezed her hand to show he was also 'listening' and between them all, she learned what had happened in the tower above them.

"*My friends can help but only if you tell your family to find a place away from falling stones.*" It appeared as if Zarleg was talking directly to Corwin.

"*He's scared. What do you want me to do?* "

Sarine caught Krass's eyes. The new voice was distinctly Dee's.

"*My friends will help but you must seek shelter from falling rocks.*" This was definitely Zarleg replying.

"What does Zarleg mean?" Sarine asked Krass.

"He has flying friends, haven't you, Zarleg? But how can they help?" Krass said.

"There is no time to explain. Please, Dee and Corwin do as I say. I have to stop talking to you so I can call my friends."

Sarine found the words and feelings in her mind abruptly cut off.

"He does that sometimes," Krass said. "We can do no more now but watch and wait."

"What for?"

"I don't really know any more than you," The elderly man gave Sarine a brief hug. "Don't be surprised at what happens but remember Zarleg is loyal to us all. He once told me that my friends are his friends."

"I hope so," Sarine whispered and moved up the track until the monastery came into view through the foliage.

*

Something like distant aeroplanes appeared high in the sky beyond the monastery. When Sarine shaded her eyes and studied the arrivals she noticed flapping wings. So they were creatures and not machines?

Eight flying creatures approached and she could now see their shape. Their heads were like gigantic ducks with orange beaks and huge searching eyes. There was a long neck but no feathers. Instead the body and wings were covered with a leathery membrane with elongated fingers on a crude hand a third of the way out of the wings. These replaced the forelegs but it was the rear legs that startled Sarine. Each creature had its legs curled around a huge boulder.

"Quetzalcoatluses," Krass muttered. "They are not normally domesticated like Zarleg and his kind."

The quetzalcoatluses were in a perfect formation with the leader being followed directly behind by the others spiralling up above it. The circle tightened until it appeared as a mammoth corkscrew above the upper monastery. Guards in the guardhouse and on an upper tower parapet were seen running into defensive positions and blue rays shot skyward.

"They won't be hurt," Krass whispered. "If anything it'll only make them angry."

He was right. The leader howled a bloodcurdling screech and dived. It came in low below the outer tower, flapped its wings, rose and crossed the building. Sarine actually saw the boulder drop, hit the tower and explode like a bomb. One whole section crumbled and fell into the valley below.

As the quetzalcoatlus flew away the second attacked. With pinpoint accuracy the boulder landed beside the first. A second section of tower wall cracked open. The third, fourth and fifth creatures flew down. Their boulders pounded the same area. The outer tower imploded in a cloud of dust, Boulders, masonry and other debris dropped down the cliff side, increased speed and an avalanche thundered into the valley below.

The sixth quetzalcoatlus flew in. The boulder dropped though the hole that was left with devastating consequences. The whole interior of the monastery exploded in a ball of orange flames that filled the sky. Seconds later, a rumble of thunder and the stench of burned fuel hit watching trio.

"They'll be killed," Sarine screamed. "Nobody can survive that explosion."

The last two quetzalcoatluses were lifted by the blast and their boulders dropped harmlessly into the valley below. But the damage had been done! Several more explosions followed the first until the whole monastery was covered in black smoke and flames that bellowed high into the air.

Zarleg roared and Sarine just stood trembling in shock.

"Stand away. Flower is coming!" His words were distinct in her mind.

Krass grabbed and almost carried her across to a nearby thicket. He lowered her down and squatted beside her, just as a quetzalcoatlus dropped and landed beside Zarleg. Even with her wings folded she was as large as the tsintaosaurus. Her beak opened and a squeaky rumble filled the air. Zarleg grumbled and waved his forepaws at the tunnel.

"Zarleg and Flower are talking," Krass whispered.

"It has a name?" Sarine couldn't stop the tremble in her voice.

"And why not?" Zarleg cut in. *"You have one. All my friends are named after beautiful items of nature. Flower is the matriarch of the flock. I'd welcome and thank her if I was you."*

"Stand up and do it," Krass hissed.

Sarine had never felt so afraid in her life but realised it was up to her. She squeezed Krass's hand and stood up, stepped out and found herself beside Flower's legs. Oh hell, the legs towered a metre over her head into a slim body that rose under folded wings. A gigantic head moved down and an eye almost as large as a wagon wheel blinked at her.

"On behalf of my human friends I wish to thank you, Flower," Sarine thought the creature would be more responsive to formal speech.

Flower's voice filled her mind. *"It went badly. We did not anticipate the fire. By themselves our rocks would have only crumbled the stone walls. I can hear the little male child crying. Your friends are safe for the moment but trapped. That is why I'm here."*

"Then get on with it Flower!" Zarleg interrupted.

Flower turned. *"Males are always impatient,"* she retorted and the one gigantic eye turned to Sarine and blinked. *"Unless you wish to stay here and fight the warriors who are even now regrouping I suggest you come with me."*

She rose, stretched her wings out above them and sort of ambled forward to straddle the wagon.

"Untie the ropes."

Krass walked across and undid the ropes holding the canvas cover and knotted the ends together. Flower grabbed the knot and rose with the wagon cover ballooning out like a parachute beneath her flapping wings.

"Climb aboard and I'll take you to them."

Zarleg stared at Krass and Sarine heard his last words. *"You have been a friend but the time has come. This is not your world, my friend so go with your own kind. I will remain here with my own."* The tsintaosaurus lowered her head beside the old man and licked him on the chin with his massive tongue. *"Perhaps when times are better you can come back and visit."*

"But where?" Krass was almost in tears as he arched his neck to look Zarleg in the eyes.

"The portal, you silly old man. You came here through one. Go with Sarine, meet the others and leave before the it fades away to nothingness."

"Come on, Krass," Sarine said and led him to the bellowing canvas. They fought the downdraft and crawled inside. Flower rose, the ends pulled up and Sarine was tossed onto Krass as they swung in a slow circle. She could see nothing but white canvas but knew they were in the air and heading for the burning monastery above.

*

Shelley grimaced when her damaged foot sent a spasm of pain up her leg when her heel touched the ground. "It's no good," she gasped.

Loretta placed an arm around her shoulders. "Crawl over there," she whispered.

Shelley nodded and tested her right knee. As long as she didn't bump her lower leg, it supported her weight. She shook tears from her eyes and crawled to the spot Loretta indicated, a gap beneath a laboratory bench. The back was covered in metal sheeting so unless someone walked directly in front of them they'd be out of sight. Loretta lay beside the bench and peeped around the edge.

"Someone's coming," she hissed.

"They're here," a harsh male voice spat. "Search the room."

Loretta slid back and tucked herself in beside Shelley. She

looked scared but attempted to cover her emotions by holding a hand over her mouth. Footsteps clumped on the wooden floor and there was the sound of objects being thrust aside, someone cursed and dust rose. They would be found within seconds!

The explosion made Shelley jump in fright. She bumped her foot and swallowed a scream at the agony from her shattered foot. Wood, stones, glass and junk howled around and a ray of sunlight appeared across the room. Everything shook as if there was an earthquake, several people screamed, a ray pistol blasted across the room and harsh orders spat out.

A loud creaking noise that followed was caused by a crack that zigzagged across the floor, which quivered and dropped in a cloud of dust. She went into a violent coughing spasm and attempted to wipe her eyes. Loretta began sneezing but otherwise, silence followed.

The dust cleared and Loretta gasped. Shelley bumped her foot, gasped as more pain shot up her leg but her attention was elsewhere, Outside the bench there was no room, just an abyss with brown dust blowing away to reveal sky ahead and trees in the valley far below.

"Oh my stars, look!" Loretta gasped.

A gigantic flying dinosaur approached. It's wings flapped in slow motion as the orange beak and hawk like eyes searched downwards. It held a massive boulder between its two legs. As it came closer a shadow cut across before Shelley. She watched, fascinated more than scared as the creature flew over and released the boulder.

It dropped ahead of them, the floor shook and she heard the roar of another explosion. Clouds of dust obliterated the view, as the rumble of moving materials became a howling roar.

Loretta clung to her. Something hit the bench above with a twang but must have bounced away for the bench remained intact. They both began coughing when dust blew in to sting eyes and hinder breathing. Before this cloud moved away, there was as third explosion, another violent shaking and another rumble of falling rocks.

"There are more," Loretta cried.

Shelley wiped her eyes again and peeped out. She saw several more gigantic creatures circling in. Every one had a boulder tucked under its body. They flew over and the dropping boulders screamed like a sirens before landing ahead of them. One more creature flew in at a slightly higher angle and Shelley saw the boulder rolling slightly as it dropped down.

This result was different! Above and behind them the whole area exploded. The sky disappeared in a ball of orange and yellow before there was an almighty bang; another earthquake and everything went black.

No it wasn't quite black! A slither of dust impregnated light cut across in front Shelley. More explosions occurred and the sounds of falling rocks continued. Something hit the top of their bench and the air stunk of scorched chemicals. Slowly, though, the nearby sounds stopped, a few objects pinged off the bench above and the distant explosions turned to a roar of fire. It was becoming hotter!

"Shelley," Loretta gasped. "We have to get out of here before the fire arrives."

"No, we're safe for the moment."

"But our air will be sucked away. We'll be asphyxiated."

"Don't panic. We're still alive and I think the fire is further up ahead of us."

"But we'll stuck here. Nobody knows where we are. We'll..." Loretta was almost panicking.

"Those creatures planned their attack," Shelley replied. "They're on our side and I wouldn't mind betting that Rhett and the others are not far away." Ignoring the pain in her foot she reached over and took Loretta's hand. "We'll wait for them to come."

"Oh Shelley," Loretta wept. "I'm sorry. You're right of course. The timing of this attack was so perfect it couldn't be a coincidence. Those flying dinosaurs must have been sent by Krass."

*

Rhett's emotions were a frenzy of despair when the explosions continued and the small passageway they were in shook continuously. He seized the children when a crack appeared on the outer wall. It widened and sunlight shone through.

"Stay back!" he screamed to Victor who had stepped forward in an almost trancelike condition as he muttered a prayer. "Whatever has happened you won't help by getting yourself killed."

Victor turned but just stood there shaking with his beard quivering. Irene rose, stepped over, placed an arm around the old man and led him back.

"He's in shock," she whispered.

Rhett nodded and looked at the children. Both were pale but their eyes retained a sparkle he didn't expect.

Another explosion sounded above them and the entire side wall sank. Where the abbot had been mere seconds before was open sky with smoke pouring across the far distance.

"The other way," Dee whispered. Her eyes turned to terror as she stared beyond Rhett. He turned.

Ahead was another gap, a long narrow one less than six centimetres wide but over two metres high. Through it, Rhett could see smoke and fire. As the smoke curled around he made out the interior of an ultramodern laboratory. People were running everywhere in a state of chaos. Some were screaming, others moaning, one had a fire extinguisher blowing carbon dioxide on a burning computer while one man dressed in a black uniform shouted orders, which were being ignored.

The voices were hushed by the background explosions but Rhett was sure the man wasn't speaking English. A shaking hand tugged on his shirt and Verton spoke.

"He's the sham who took my place. I recognise some of the others, too."

"The fake priests?"

Verton nodded.

Their conversation was interrupted by another explosion, so loud Rhett's ears rung. Smoke poured through the gap, putrid black smoke that left them all coughing and gasping for breath. White light flickered through the blackness and for several moments, he concentrated on protecting the children. He flung his coat over both Dee and Corwin and pulled them into his arms while Irene helped Victor. They huddled together as the smoke bellowed over them. Luckily, most if it blew out into the abyss beyond.

The shaking stopped and Rhett glanced through the crack again. The room beyond was no more! Everything had gone! Even the explosion had imploded into nothingness with the fire extinguished as if a giant finger had snuffed it out. As quickly as it arrived the smoke dissipated into the blue sky above. There was no upper chamber for the entire tower had vanished and apparently killed everyone within it.

…Except them!

"Goddess Arianrhod has destroyed the evil ones and helped us," Verton muttered.

Rhett was angry. "And what about Shelley?' he howled. "Why has your goddess killed her and Loretta, too? They're not evil!"

"Daddy," Dee shouted. "She's alive or we wouldn't be here either, now would we?"

Of course! Rhett gasped, seized his daughter and kissed her cheek. He turned, grabbed Corwin and also kissed him as emotion burst through his mind.

"She's below us, Daddy," Corwin whispered. "Mummy's safe." He glanced up. "Her leg is sore but she is safe. Loretta is looking after her."

"Corwin's right, Daddy," Dee cried. "Can't you hear her?"

Rhett frowned. He listened but all he could hear was distant rumbling. Rocks must be still sliding down the cliff. But, wait a moment... oh my God... Dee was right! Outside and below he heard a voice. Her voice!

Rhett squeezed the children so hard they gasped, stood up and shouted. "Shelley!" Can you hear me, Shelley?"

"Rhett!" Her voice was definitely below them. "Is that you?"

"Help us, please!" That was Loretta's voice. "We're trapped!"

"I'll take you to them," Corwin whispered in a confident voice. "I know where Mummy is."

*

The stairs Corwin led them down had not been damaged and it was Dee whose forehead creased into a pout as they continued down. She slid in beside Rhett and grabbed his hand.

"These are the stairs I went up to find you," she said.

"What do you mean, Dee?" Rhett was so worried about Shelley he wasn't really listening.

"When we first met," Dee said. "Somewhere out there is the ledge where the portal is. Once we get Mum we can go out and get to it." Her eyes stared intently at him. "We've found what we were looking for, Dad. I'm positive this is the same place."

They came to a landing with a doorway off to the left while the stairs continued down on the right. Corwin turned, ran up to the door and threw it open.

"Rhett!" Shelley's voice was close. "We're under a laboratory bench."

"It's probably covered in rocks," Loretta added.

Across the room the ceiling had collapsed but amongst the debris, Rhett saw the end of a long metal bench. Crumpled plaster and debris covered one side while the other end was flattened by a mountain of rocks and bricks.

"Goddess Arianrhod has helped," Abbot Verton whispered. "She stopped the wall collapsing over them."

Rhett tore forward, heaved junk aside and found a slab of plaster covering an open space.

"Shelley!"

"We're in here, Rhett," Shelley replied. "Oh my stars, how did you find us?"

"Corwin knew where to come," Rhett cried as he seized the plaster with both hands and pulled it aside.

*

CHAPTER TWELVE

The best way to carry Shelley was by piggyback. She had her hands clasped around Rhett's neck and her legs through his arms as he followed Dee along the track. It was scary rather than dangerous with the skeletal remains of the tower on the left and loose rubble dropping away to the right. Immediately behind the pair were Victor, Corwin and the two women.

The area smelt of scorched earth but all that remained of the fire were isolated pockets of smoke that would occasionally burst into flame. There was no tower but, further back, the rest of the monastery with the two other towers appeared blackened but relatively unscathed by the explosions.

"Dad." Dee stopped and turned slightly to face her father. "The portal looks different?"

From the side the portal appeared like a framework standing alone on the inside of the track. Behind it was rubble and the cliff.

"It's like the one in your kitchen at Riversdale," Shelley said. "I guess that over the years the inside filled up to become part of the cliff."

"But that's definitely it," Rhett said. "I'll be glad to get there. Your mum is pretty heavy, Dee."

"I am not," Shelley pulled her wrists in and almost throttled him.

"Strong too," he muttered after he could breath again.

"Stop, something's wrong," Victor interrupted.

Rhett obeyed. He studied the portal and the surrounding area but could see nothing different. Until now he had concentrated on the object itself and had not looked beyond it. When he did he saw what had attracted Victor's attention. A man was partly hidden by the portal frame.

Victor's warning was, however, too late. The man stepped out in front of the portal. His uniform was charred, one side of his face blistered and he wore no cap. The uniform, though was recognisable, black, ominous and with a red armband containing a swastika. If they weren't in such a precarious situation, Rhett would have laughed at the theatrical appearance. It reminded him of an old war movie that thrilled him as a kid.

"Es, ist Verräter der Menschheit weit genug," the man screamed and aimed a ray pistol at them.

"He said, 'That's far enough, traitors of humanity.'" Shelley whispered in his ear. "Be careful."

"It's Dedrik Jaeger," Victor's voice quivered. "He's a sadistic psychopath and probably the real leader. He also speaks English as well as we do."

"Okay," Rhett whispered and turned towards the man. "We are not responsible for the destruction here. All we wish to do is go back to our world."

"Liar!" Jaeger replied. "That woman you carry is a traitor who has sided with the reptilian creatures trying to destroy humanity." He raised his weapon. "You may have won this first battle but I will not allow the bitch to destroy all that is right in our worlds."

Rhett swallowed anger but his mind was a whirl about what to do. If he dropped Shelley and charged he might reach him before... No that was stupid.

"Let the children go," he said in an enforced calm voice. "They have hurt nobody."

Jaeger hesitated and cast his eyes over Dee and Corwin. "Nice specimens," he almost whispered. "Yours?"

Dee's voice filled Rhett's mind.

"Zarleg, we're in trouble. We need your friends to help us? Now!"

"Coming. Play for time," came an immediate reply.

"Yes they are my children," he replied.

"Who's the mother?"

Shelley squeezed a warning. Perhaps... "Loretta here, is," he lied and nodded at the blonde girl behind them.

"Get her to step forward."

Loretta nodded and caught Rhett's eyes as she squeezed past him. She took a step forward and stood there visibly afraid.

"These your children?" Jaeger barked.

"Yes."

"And you're from Earth?"

"My parents were."

"And you have an ancestry tree to show your purity?"

Rhett felt ill at the thought that this bigotry had survived for centuries.

"I believe so," Loretta said.

"You believe!" Jaeger screamed. "You believe. Why you're as bad as the rest. You should know! Anybody who does not know their pure ancestry going back five generations does not deserve to live."

"Our family records were deleted when our spaceship was destroyed," Loretta replied, perhaps a little too hastily. "I should have said I know but cannot prove my ancestry."

The ray gun lowered slightly. "You appear physically pure."

"Keep going, Loretta" Rhett whispered.

Dee's hand touched his. "Dad!" she whispered.

Rhett didn't want to take his eyes off Jaeger but discretely moved his focus beyond the man. One of the flying dinosaurs was dropping in from out of the sky.

"Can I bring the children to you?" Loretta said.

"If you come, your husband will not be needed."

"Don't argue with him," Shelley whispered. "Smile as if you agree."

"Of course. I understand," Loretta called out and provocatively wriggled her hips. "Perhaps we could work together."

"Work?" Jaeger laughed. "I don't normally call it work. However, I like your idea. Bring the children forward with you and their lives will be spared. I..."

A shadow flashed across the track, the man turned, screamed in sheer terror and raised his weapon. He was not aiming at them though, but at the gigantic duckbill faced flying monster that descended upon him.

It was over within seconds. The gigantic bill opened, let out a terrifying screech and seized the Nazi in its bill. The pistol in his hand spun away out of sight into the abyss below. The bill chomped and the following scream was from Jaeger's mouth as he was lifted, kicking and gyrating into the air. His howl cut off abruptly as blood squirted from the creature's mouth. Wings flapped and it circled away above them.

"Rhett!" Shelley cried and almost throttled him again.

About a hundred metres above them, Jaeger's head, arms and upper body dropped in a line of bloody spittle. His legs were still in the creature's mouth. He had been bitten in half! The creature swallowed and the legs disappeared.

"It ate his legs!" Loretta screamed.

"Yes," Rhett replied. "I'm glad that creature's on our side."

"Daddy," Corwin cried. "Another one!"

Rhett turned. Another creature was circling in but this one was coming up from the valley below. He frowned. Something was in its mouth, a sort of rucksack held at the top and carrying something inside. It flew up and around on a flight path similar to the earlier creature. When it was close the downdraft almost blew them backwards as it hovered and the head moved down. Oh my God, two people were lying inside the rucksack.

"It's the wagon cover," Shelley cried. "It's got the canvas in its mouth."

The canvas touched the ground and flattened out. From inside a woman crawled out, closely followed by an elderly man. Both clung to a piece of rock and staggered to their feet, just as the creature flew up and away.

"Thank you Flower," Sarine shouted and waved. She turned, placed an arm around Krass to support him and stepped forward. "I believe you all had a spot of trouble," she said.

*

Emotions came to the fore as Loretta and Irene ran forward and hugged Sarine. She just held her friends and burst into shuddering tears.

"He was an animal," she cried. "Worse than animal, an insect..."

Krass glanced around. "You're all here! That's wonderful." He turned and squinted at the abbot. "I know you, don't I?"

Victor reached out and took his hand. "Yes. A few years back we met. Remember I tried to get you to stay with us in the monastery and when you refused, I allowed you to use the lower one."

"Of course. You're Abbot One!"

"I was but call me Victor."

As the conversation moved on, Rhett studied the surrounding area. There appeared to be two vulnerable spots, the track they had come along from the collapsed tower and the area beyond the portal where the track disappeared around a distant corner.

"We're exposed here. I suggest we get through the portal as soon as we can." He turned to face everyone as he hitched Shelley higher up on his back. "I assume you're all coming."

"Zarleg persuaded me," Krass replied.

"I can't," Victor replied.

"Of course you can," Shelley began." This is not a human world. We can find..."

Victor just smiled slightly. "And my monks? They must be in the monastery below. Do we just leave them?"

"They can come, too," Dee cut in.

"No. I believe this portal is unstable. It may vanish within an hour, perhaps even minutes. The evil ones are either all dead or powerless and my duty is to serve my monks and goddess. She saved us all so who am I, a mere mortal, to abandon her in this hostile world."

"And you believe she is real?" Shelley whispered.

"My monks do," Victor whispered. "Myself?" He shrugged. "It is difficult to place the beliefs of a lifetime aside. Perhaps you are her personification, Shelley."

"Me. Why me!"

Victor smiled. "Your foot for one."

Rhett glanced at Shelley's leg that was across his stomach. Oh hell, it had been a pulpy bloody mess but the swelling had gone. In fact her skin appeared smooth with her bare toes wriggling in front of a perfectly formed foot.

"Let me down, Sweetheart," Shelley whispered.

He lowered her onto her good leg. She hopped for a moment before placing her wounded foot to the ground. She shifted her weight onto it and smiled. "It's tender but doesn't hurt," she whispered as she stepped back to Victor. She flung her arms around him and kissed him quite passionately on the cheek. "Please come with us," she said.

"I made my choice," Victor replied. "I am needed here and your journey has not been completed. Sometime in the future I believe our paths will cross again." He kissed her cheek, hugged the others and stepped back along the track. "Now go, my children, before the portal closes and you have to serve your lives out in this remote corner of space-time."

"Come on." Rhett whispered.

He guided them forward like a shepherd with a flock of sheep, watched as they entered a tiny room through the portal and stood back to wave at the abbot.

"Rhett!" Shelley screamed.

Rhett turned to see the portal and everyone within becoming wobbly and transparent. He saw a hand extended, grabbed it and bolted forward into Shelley's arms.

"Don't you ever do that to me," she sobbed and kissed him.

He spun around. Through the door he could only see a red and yellow spinning universe backed by infinite blackness of deep space. It disappeared to reveal the interior of a gigantic spacecraft sort of hovering off the cliff face.

"I've seen something like this before. It's a gigantic three dimensional monitor," Shelley gasped.

Rhett watched, fascinated as the scene before them played out.

*

"Rear Admiral Shelley Medina on the Bridge," shouted a master of arms sergeant. The hundreds of assembled officers and crew standing in rows ahead, all snapped to rigid attention while a grim looking man dressed in a formal white uniform showing the stars of a captain on his lapel, saluted.

"Everyone including the auxiliary crew are here as ordered, Rear Admiral," he said in clipped words. "Robotic guard personnel are operating all battle stations."

Shelley gasped at the view. The woman was dressed in a white admiralty uniform with the large gold star and two smaller stars on her lapel and gold brads on her jacket arm. But the Rear Admiral who returned the captain's salute looked familiar! She gulped and looked closer. The rear admiral on the screen had short grey hair and a face with wrinkles of a fifty-year-old. She still looked slim and fit and the eyes held an expression of someone tired or even exhausted but somehow Shelley guessed that this was not one of her ancestors or descendants, it was herself but how she would be in twenty-five years.

"The assembled crew can relax, sergeant," Rear Admiral Medina said.

"Stand at... Ease!" the sergeant shouted.

Like one, feet shot outward and hands moved behind each person in the less formal position.

"They can sit, sergeant,"

"Sit Ma'am?" the sergeant looked appalled.

"You heard!"

The sergeant snapped to attention, saluted and turned with his heels clicking. "Assembly!" he roared. "Rear Admiral Shelley Medina orders you all to sit..." He swallowed. "Sit!" he screamed as if the order was beneath his dignity.

Everyone did and a murmur filtered through the crew.

"Silence!" screamed the Master of Arms.

Shelley watched the older version of herself wait a few seconds before she began to speak.

"I have grave news that is only being released to you all because, in spite of the dedicated service and indeed bravery by you all, we may lose our present battle. You all know that our illustrious name Battlecruiser Sif comes from ancient Norse Earth Alpha mythology where Sif was the consort of Thor, the god of thunder and battle. May this help us in the impending engagement with the girifa but I'm afraid the odds are against us.

The eight girifa battlecruisers that surround our ship may appear to be but they are not, however, our real enemy...The real enemy are as human as you and I." When she paused, the only sound was a faint whirr of air conditioning as every person aboard clung to her words. "This enemy is not from our universe but a parallel one, which we have designated System Sigma. On Earth Sigma, history of the mid 20th century went on a tangent to our own. In that world, the Nazi Germans produced an atomic bomb in 1943. They used this weapon with devastating consequences in 1944. Moscow, London, Manchester and New York were hit by atomic bombs and destroyed.

The allies surrendered on Christmas Day 1944 and the world was ruled for the next century by the evil philosophy known as Nazism.

My orders from the very beginning, ladies and gentlemen, has been to find and either destroy this society or block all access between this parallel world and our own."

The scene faded and changed to the fifty-year old Shelley sitting behind a modernistic desk. Rear Admiral Medina's tired eyes lifted and appeared to bore right into Shelley. "This recording and the one you have just viewed can only be activated by my DNA from future or past space-time," she whispered. "I was told it might be you and not myself who saves human and girifa life as we know it. I hope you succeed where I failed. "

"There's more," he whispered. "Listen!"

The older Shelley on the screen continued. "Use your earrings if you wear them. As you may have already found out, they are more than decorations. Thrust them again." She smiled. "You are, whether you wish it or not, my backup plan to succeed where I failed."

Rear Admiral Medina gave a half salute and the monitor faded to show the original view of deep space. This, in turn faded to reveal the portal which they had just walked through.

"Mum," Dee gasped as the room itself dissolved to reveal a small rock cavity around them and nothing else.

"So the only purpose of this portal was give you that message," Rhett whispered. He glanced at Shelley. "I'd say your older self has been stringing us along."

"What do you mean, Rhett?"

"Oh, I don't know." Rhett whispered as he tucked his arms around her. "I am beginning to feel like a pawn on a chess board, that's all."

"No Rhett," Krass replied. "I'd say we are the knights on that chessboard you mentioned with moves in more than one direction. We need to be careful when we plan this next move, that's all."

"There's no choice at the moment," Shelley muttered. "We have to go out the portal again."

*

As soon as they walked back out onto the ledge, Shelley could see changes. The foremost one was the rubble that looked weathered and solid with grass and other vegetation growing through cracks. The track appeared unused and stained by rusty watermarks. Everything had the appearance of having been there for years.

They made their way back to the top of the stairs. Rhett offered to go down first but was outvoted so en masse, they walked down through deserted floors until they reached the entrance. Everything was deserted and had been unused for years. The lower floors were still intact but contained no furniture. A few signs of vandalism with broken windows and faded graffiti painted on walls also appeared old. Dust competed with cobwebs as the dominant feature of the rooms and a musty smell impregnated the building.

The outside was similar. There was no guardhouse or cutting but only a rubble-filled ditch with two metre high trees in it replaced the original cutting.

"Ten years or more," Rhett muttered almost to himself as he picked up a piece of rotting guard rail and tossed it away. "It's like the monastery when you arrived isn't it, Dee?"

Like the others, his daughter had been studying everything around with a concentrated gaze. "No," she whispered, "It's the same place but there are differences."

"Like what, Sweetheart?" Shelley asked.

"Little things... the trees for example. I can't remember seeing them growing close nor did I notice the remains of the cutting they're in. The stairs are different, too. I'm sure I went straight up without going out onto different floors."

"We're on a home world," Corwin added.

"Home world?" Rhett asked. "What do you mean, Corwin?"

"Look!" The boy pointed up above the forest below.

Rhett followed the direction Corwin indicated. Riding an updraft in the distance were two circling birds, hawks or other birds of prey by the look of them.

Krass frowned. "There were no birds in my world," he said. "You have keen eyesight, Lad."

Corwin flushed at the compliment. "I noticed birds nests in the room upstairs, too and rats."

"What?" screeched Dee,

"There was a large rat running between some rocks."

"It wasn't a lizard?' Krass asked.

"No," Loretta said. "I saw it too."

The situation was even more mystifying after they walked down the zigzag to the valley below. There was no lower monastery, not even ruins but about two hundred metres along the track was a wagon.

"My wagon," Krass gasped. "Look it even lacks the canvas cover. We took it off so Flower could carry us up to meet you."

He was right! Everything was there from clothes to food, which was fresh!

Irene glanced at Sarine and the pair disappeared through the trees. Rhett noticed them go but was more interested in examining the wagon. That was until the pair returned a few moments later leading a giant Clydesdale horse. The lumbering animal whinnied and walked right up to Krass who rubbed his nose.

"I know you, don't I?' he said in a strange voice. He turned to Rhett. "I was never religious or superstitious but this has me beat."

"It's logical, though," Irene said. "If we're back in a world of animals instead of reptiles, something would have needed to pull the wagon."

"But not Zarleg," Krass whispered. He stroked the horse's mane. "This is Zarleg. He was transported to this new world, too but couldn't be here as a tsintaosaurus so they changed him."

"Who's 'they'?" Shelley asked.

"The same ones who fixed your foot and talked to us in that movie."

"My older self?" Shelley gasped.

"Possibly but I don't think so."

"Well, it certainly wasn't that goddess Victor worshipped," Loretta retorted.

"And why not?" Krass retorted.

"It's just mythology. They don't exist!"

"When I grew up on twenty-first century Earth we didn't know of other worlds," Rhett said. "In fact, most scientists believed that if there were other living beings in other galaxies, they'd be so far away we'd never be able to contact them anyway."

"Most civilisations create stories to explain things they don't understand," Irene added.

"So Victor's Goddess Arianrhod could be based on some advanced life force that visited their world?" Shelley asked.

Rhett shrugged. "It's as logical as any other explanation. Perhaps that rear admiral was just a fragment of our imagination."

"Placed there to motivate us into doing what they wish?" Shelley whispered.

"Whoever or whatever they are, they seem to want us alive," Krass glanced at the sky. "It's mid-afternoon. Unless we find something better to do, I suggest we set up camp for the night and head off to find a village in the morning."

"You think there'll be one?" Dee asked.

Krass nodded. "The wagon, the horse and a road on which to travel means it must lead to and from places that people need to travel between."

Rhett grinned. "But we keep an eye out around us," he said. "There could be human savages out there, you know."

"There aren't," Corwin said. "Nobody around will hurt us."

Rhett believed the little boy. Every time he'd made a statement, it had proved to be correct. Dee caught his eyes and smiled. "It's a completely new world, Dad," she said. "Of that, I am sure."

*

CHAPTER THIRTEEN

The land the eight travellers found themselves in could have been southern Europe or western United States in the nineteenth century. For six weeks, they followed the tracks and minor roads through the land in their wagon that was now equipped with a new canvas cover they'd managed to purchase in one of the villages they'd travelled through. It was summer with the days warm and signs of grass growth everywhere. The villagers were olive skinned, dark haired peaceful people who wore old-fashioned clothes and lived in wooden or stone dwellings built haphazardly around a central square, consisting of a handful of commercial buildings, a school and a market.

The third village, where they had been for three weeks, was surrounded by massive vegetable gardens and fruit trees. Everyone, included the children, picked fruit, strawberries and gathered pumpkins while the men helped dig potatoes and other heavier work in this, the harvest season. It was strenuous physical work but they all became fit and tanned by the sun.

Communication was mainly through Krass who was the only one who could understand the local language. Shelley and Dee's earrings remained silent and there was no telepathy evident at all. The new Zarleg was a gentle giant horse who, if anything, was lazier than the tsintaosaurus from 'the other side' that they had begun to call the world they'd come from. With the bronze coins they'd earned for their work, Krass purchased items from the market that could be resold at the next village while the women stocked up their food supply and clothing.

"I hate these long dresses," Dee moaned as she swung around in her ankle length dress.

"I know," Shelley replied. "But you must admit they do keep you cool and stop the locals staring at us."

"Yeah! But they still stare at us, Mum. It happens all the time."

"That's the trouble," Loretta, also dressed in a local gown said. "I don't trust the men."

Shelley glanced across the community hut they lived in. "Why, has something happened?"

"No," Irene said. "But if we stay any longer it will."

Even the modest Sarine agreed. "I think we should move on before there is a challenge."

"What's that?"

"The younger men will challenge Rhett's right to have four women under his care. You've seen those wrestling matches that go on in the square once a week?"

Shelley nodded. It was one aspect of village life she didn't like.

"They are all about the women. Rhett will be challenged and if he loses a fight he will have to forfeit one of us to the winner."

"But we aren't Rhett's property!" Irene gasped.

"The villagers believe we are all his wives and Krass our father. It is not an unusual local arrangement."

Shelley frowned. She'd also felt uncomfortable at times when she was working or shopping in the market but hadn't suspected it was so bad. "How do you know this?"

"I've learned their language," Sarine said. "The locals don't realise this and talk freely in front of us. I picked up most of this news from the women when we're down washing clothes in the stream."

Later that day, Shelley cornered Krass on the edge of the pumpkin field and told him about the situation. He sighed and nodded. "I have already been approached," he said.

"What?"

"It is true that they think of all you women as Rhett's wives, not that that concept really applies here. Family life here is a very loose arrangement. The children belong to everyone..." Krass flushed. "So do the women. Only older men like myself have a say in who lives together. I was offered a hundred coins for Loretta. Apparently, her blonde hair is an attraction. I refused but that challenge is coming up. I spoke to Rhett about it."

"And didn't tell us!" Shelley retorted.

Krass shrugged. "We didn't want you to worry."

"Well I am!" Shelley whispered. "We all are!"

"Which is why we leave this evening," Krass said. "Normally, visitors depart at dawn so, with luck we'll be well away before anyone realises."

He nodded out along the path where Zarleg was ambling towards them with the wagon behind. She could see Rhett in the driver's seat with Dee beside him.

"Our excuse for bringing the wagon this far out is to take a load of pumpkins back to the village," Krass said. "Actually, we've got everything packed in the back and are all ready to go."

"You could have told me!" Shelley was annoyed.

"It was Rhett who..."

"And damn him, too," Shelley cried. "What right has he to speak for me?"

"Probably none but at a rough guess I'd say it is because he loves you."

"Oh!" Shelley almost bit her tongue and reached out and squeezed Krass's arm. "I'm sorry. Somehow it was easier when we knew who the enemy like that fake abbot really were."

"The villagers aren't enemy, Shelley. In their mind they are doing nothing wrong. It is just the way it is. We are highly respected here." He raised his eyebrows. "If we weren't this would have happened not long after our arrival."

The wagon arrived and Shelley stood glaring at Rhett with her hands on her hips.

"Now what have I done?" he asked.

"I know about the challenge and everything else, Rhett," she whispered.

Rhett frowned and switched his eyes to Krass. "You told her?"

"No. Sarine did," the old man replied.

"She learned their language but didn't let on," Shelley continued. "She overheard the women talking."

"And where is she and the others?" Rhett asked.

"Across the field. I wanted to talk to Krass alone. You have both children?"

"I'm here, Mum." Corwin popped his head out of the new canvas cover behind Dee.

"So we leave now," Rhett replied. "If we go back to the village I'll be challenged and we'll all be stopped from leaving."

"And how do you know that?" Shelley whispered.

Rhett almost smiled. "I'm not as good as Sarine, I admit but I've also picked up some of the local language. In some ways it is like ancient English, you know in syntax and many of the words, such as haas for horse? Like her, I just listened. It was all the talk when I was in the tavern at lunchtime."

"Rhett!" Shelley retorted. "I told you not to go in there."

"Now who's being bossy?" Krass whispered.

Shelley felt her face burn with embarrassment. "I'm sorry. It's just too long. I don't want to spend my whole life in this primitive world." She swung around. "I'll go and get the others."

As she walked through the winding path between the pumpkins she felt as if every man working there was staring at her. The relaxed gentle atmosphere had been replaced by a sinister overtone. She brushed her long skirt down and ignored the covert gazes.

Loretta, Irene and Sarine came up to her.

"It's all on, isn't it?" Sarine asked.

Shelley nodded. "Just keep working and pile the pumpkins up at the end of each row. We'll make our way slowly back to the wagon."

*

To anybody watching, it looked as if they were loading the wagon. Actually, pumpkins were being passed under the canvas to where Dee, Corwin and Loretta handed them along and out the back. From there, Sarine tossed them across to Irene standing in a dry ditch behind knee high grass. She was hidden from the field by the wagon. Unless someone walked directly to the ditch edge, the pumpkins would remain hidden.

Zarleg ambled forward to the next row, the others followed and

Irene crouched as she made her way along the ditch. The manoeuvre was repeated a second and third time until Krass called a halt.

"Make a pile of pumpkins at the back and crouch down behind them. Rhett you drive and let Dee sit beside you. She always does this so it will not seem unusual. I'll stroll along the track beside you."

"Why don't we just go?" Shelley asked.

"We have to go by that far tool shed." Krass nodded to a small building at the edge of the field. "There are always men gathered around there having a gossip. Today there are more than usual."

"Why?"

Krass hesitated.

"Tell her, Krass," Rhett said.

The old man nodded. "The whole village knows about the upcoming challenges. They're going to have a preliminary competition. Bets are being placed on who wins this. The winner will then challenge Rhett who, incidentally, nobody expects to win."

"Go on," hissed Shelley.

"Loretta and you are the women they want. After beating Rhett, the winner will be allowed to pick which of you he wants and the other one will given to the guy who came second. Rhett will be allowed to choose between Sarine or Irene to keep and the one he doesn't choose will be fought for."

"Fought for?" Irene gasped.

"A junior competition for the younger men. Usually, any girl who has just come of age is the prize. Apparently, there are none this week."

"And how old is that?" Loretta gasped.

Krass shrugged. "They're picked by the women by their physical maturity, not age as we recognise it."

Shelley noticed that she and the others looked as horrified as she felt. "So we get out," she whispered.

*

The women's absence from the pumpkins would be noticed if anybody searched but that was one risk they'd have to take. Rhett held the reins grimly as Zarleg plodded by the hut. There were seven or eight men there who stared at him and grinned. As Rhett listened, anger rose in his throat. Two younger guys were not looking at him but at Dee.

"I don't care if you win tomorrow's junior fight, Pars and pick one of the old girls. I'm waiting for next week's competition," a tall skinny boy almost sniggered.

"Why, Flanz?"

"Next week the men are classifying Dee there as a woman." He laughed and shouted at Dee. "You'll be mine babe!"

"Shut up!" Pars retorted.

"They don't understand us. Just smile and she'll think we're asking if it's a nice day." He waved at Dee who frowned and turned to Rhett.

"Daddy, I don't like this. Why is he looking at me that way?"

"A few more moments, Dee. Don't show any fear. Just smile and wave at them."

Krass must have sized up the situation for he strolled forward and grabbed Flanz by the arm, stared him straight in the eyes and spat out a stiletto of words. The boy, hesitated, looked away and muttered something.

"Well, do it!" Krass shouted in English.

The boy nodded, glanced at one of the older men who shrugged, and ran off back towards the village. Pars glanced at Krass and stepped away.

"I told him to run back to the village and tell the women to prepare a meal as we'd be back soon," Krass called up. "You'd better stop the wagon."

Rhett grimaced but pulled Zarleg to a halt. "What is it?" he hissed.

"The guy I just spoke to wants to talk. If I let you just keep going it will seem suspicious. I won't be long." Krass glanced at Dee. "Chin up, Dee," he said. "You're doing well."

Dee nodded but still looked apprehensive as Krass walked into the shed and disappeared behind a closed door. Rhett waited and tried to remain expressionless.

Dee glanced at Flanz who was still by the shed. She smiled and caught the boy's eyes. Suddenly, to Rhett's surprise she spoke to the boy.

"Are you going to be at the market before the fights?" she asked.

Flanz turned also looked surprised and replied with a slightly embarrassed look on his face. "Might be." he replied in broken English.

Dee beamed. "See you there! Perhaps we could have a vardo." This was a low alcohol version of the adult's vardi drink. Both were made from fermented pumpkins.

"Vardo?" Flanz smiled. "Okay. Old man no mind?"

Dee shrugged. "Dad's easy. Mum's the one to talk around,"

Flanz probably didn't understand everything she said but relaxed and grinned.

Krass returned, climbed up beside the pair and took the reins. He shook them and waved to the group as the horse moved off.

"What was that about, Dee?" Rhett hissed when they were out of earshot.

"I can act too, Dad and I know what's it's all about," She frowned. "I'm not a kid anymore."

"You were taking a risk?" Rhett replied with anger in his voice.

"Was I?" Dee whispered. "That guy who was walking around the wagon came back to listen to us. All he had to do was peep through the gaps in the pumpkins at the back and he would have seen everything inside."

Rhett grimaced. She was right, of course. "I'm sorry, Sweetheart," he said. "I should have realised."

"That's okay, Dad," Dee said. "Mum gets mad if you treat her like a dummy. Sometimes you think I'm no older than Corwin. We're in this together, aren't we?" She glanced across at Krass. "So what happened to you?"

"Nothing new. I just babbled on about nothing in particular and told them it would take two more days to harvest all the pumpkins. I don't think they were suspicious."

"But don't they realise you know about everything," Rhett asked.

"They clam up when I'm around." Krass shook the reins and managed to get Zarleg going a little faster. "They did say the men were having a meeting at five and it was important that you and I attend."

"The challenge?"

"Yep! I said that was fine, we'd be there." Krass squinted ahead. "The fun is about to begin. When we get to the road, I'm turning left away from the village towards the eastern hills."

"But shouldn't we take the other road out?"

"No time," Krass said. "Once we're out of town we can change direction at that crossroads and end up going north. Isn't that the way you want to go?"

Rhett nodded. They'd come from the south and as far as he knew there was only barren land to the west.

"Okay," he said. "Dee, will you get back and tell Mum and the others to be ready? They're to hang on for it might be a rough ride."

"Not as bad as when Zarleg was a tsintaosaurus, Dad. At least we haven't got girifa warriors with spears chasing us," Dee said and disappeared back through the canvas.

*

Zarleg's gallop was more of a lumbering trot but it was still faster than that of the handful of runners who attempted to follow them. The cultivated farms soon petered into grassland dotted with low umbrella shaped trees and small shingle streams flowing down from the hills.

After almost an hour, Krass pulled Zarleg to a halt beside a stream and jumped down from the wagon. "You've done well, My Friend." He unharnessed the horse from the wagon and led him across to have a drink.

Rhett walked back along the track, it couldn't really be classified as a road, and searched the land behind them. It appeared empty. He felt arms through his and glanced back.

"What now, Rhett?" Shelley asked.

Rhett shrugged. "Perhaps we did everything wrong."

"By coming this way?"

"No, our whole journey. Think back to the monastery and the portal. We assumed that it went nowhere after seeing that video or whatever it was. But didn't we go through it before? If we'd just waited and tried again it might have opened back home."

"But we were in a parallel world. Here, we're at least in a world of humans."

"But it is not Earth. We might have moved across to an entirely different dimension."

"Dimension?" Shelley screwed her nose up.

"Well your earrings don't work here, Krass can't talk to Zarleg and the children are only that... children with no special knowledge or powers."

"And that's bad?"

"If we were back home on Earth I'd say no. I'd love to be just an ordinary family again."

Shelley glanced up at him. "We never were an ordinary family. Rhett. Any return to your ordinary Earth would be just you in that lonely little cabin. I wouldn't be there."

Rhett hugged her close and kissed her softly on the lips. "You know what I mean?"

"Yes. This place is a sort of anonymity, somewhere safe but a side journey. So you think we should return to the monastery and try the portal again?"

"After all this time, I don't know. It would be risky going back through the village."

"So let's make a time limit, say a week. If nothing happens in that time we go back. I'm sure we can find a way around the village."

They returned to the wagon to find Sarine was already setting out something to eat while the children waded in the stream.

"A lonely land." Irene appeared to have the same concerns as them.

"But better than our fate in the village," Loretta replied.

"So we keep going?" Krass studied Rhett who nodded. "And if the next village is no different or even worse?"

"I don't know," Rhett admitted. "Shelley suggests we place a time limit..."

All the adults joined in the conversation with many were scenarios raised from the amount of food they had, what could happen if they came to another village, the weather changed, the road fizzled out to desert or if someone got ill ... Finally, they came back to Shelley's idea but reduced it to three days. If nothing happened by then they would return to the monastery, a journey of at least two weeks without stopping at villages.

The children returned and lightened the atmosphere with their chatter about their fun in the stream.

"We'll leave in half an hour," Krass said. "Zarleg has rested up and we can probably put another five hours behind us before we'll need to set up camp for the night. I think we're still too close to the village for comfort."

*

It was dawn two days later. Shelley couldn't sleep so she crawled out from under the canvas awning and wandered down to the nearby stream. It was going to be another hot day with a cloudless sky. She bathed her face and wandered out to the track they had pulled off from. Since leaving the village they had seen nobody or any signs of human occupation. The land looked fertile so perhaps there were not many people in this world.

She glanced back and frowned for there appeared to be a dust cloud in the distance. Could somebody be coming? She hastened back to the wagon and shook Rhett.

"Come and look," she whispered.

Rhett was immediately awake. He threw his one blanket aside and followed her out. The cloud of dust was closer and in the centre was a small object.

"Get Krass," Rhett said.

"I'm here," the old man said. "Somebody's riding a horse." He frowned and squinted in the dim light. "Probably only one so I doubt if it's someone deliberately following us."

"I'll awaken the others," Shelley said.

A few moments later everyone was up and watching as the distant figure came closer. There was nowhere to hide the wagon but Shelley asked Irene to take the children behind a thicket across the stream.

The figure took shape. A man was riding a small horse or donkey. He travelled slowly and his slumped appearance looked like someone who was tired or even asleep in the saddle.

"Mum," Dee cried from behind her.

"Dee," Shelley cried. "I told you to remain hidden."

"But Mum, don't you see who that guy is?"

Shelley stared out. The figure did look familiar but she couldn't place him.

"It's one of those boys we overheard by the pumpkin shed; the quiet one. Wasn't his name Pars?"

Rhett nodded. "You stay back, Dee," he said. "I'll go and see what he wants."

"I'm coming with you," Shelley said.

She stepped out onto the road and found Rhett, Krass and Loretta with her. Dee was out of sight.

The donkey appeared bedraggled and as tired as its mount. The boy looked up and gasped as if he hadn't seen them until that moment.

"I found you, " he said. "When I lost your wagon wheel marks on the gravel I though I must have gone the wrong way."

"You're the boy who was making nasty comments about my daughter. Why have you followed us?" Rhett asked in a stern voice.

"I'm Pars." The boy sat swaying on the donkey and appeared exhausted. "It wasn't me. I'd never hurt Dee. She's a great kid. Anyway, Flanz is all talk."

"Go easy on him," Shelley whispered.

"No, it's okay," Pars gazed at the ground. "Flanz told the elders I had warned you about the challenge and I was called to a meeting."

"But you didn't!" Sarine had overheard the women talking."

Pars shrugged. "The elders didn't believe me and I was punished for disloyalty to the village."

"How?" Shelley whispered.

Pars turned away as tears formed in his eyes. He turned and lifted his shirt. His back was criss-crossed with lines of ugly bloodstained welts. "Eight lashes with the whip," he whispered. "I was told that I was let off lightly. If I was a year older I would have got twenty-three."

"Oh my stars," Shelley was horrified. "They did that to you just because they suspected you helped us?"

"New women are needed to improve the stock. The men..."

"We knew about the challenge." Shelley paled. "Come on Pars, we'll tend to your back. If it's not cleaned up..." She took his arm and led him over to the wagon.

*

CHAPTER FOURTEEN

Within moments Irene had a bowl of hot broth in Pars' hands while he straddled a chair with his shirt off so Sarine and Loretta could clean up his back. He did not complain even though his wounds would have stung when touched. Rhett helped Krass tend to the donkey and wandered back to Shelley with a thoughtful expression on his face.

"Okay, what's wrong?" she asked.

"A few things don't add up. For one, how come he understands us and speaks perfect English? At that pumpkin field shed he was speaking his own language and I was sure he could barely understand us."

"Perhaps my earrings helped."

"But they've been dormant ever since we've arrived here."

"So I'll ask him," Shelley said. As she walked across to the boy, her eyes settled on the saddlebag that Krass had unloaded from the donkey and placed against a wagon wheel.

"What's in your saddlebag, Pars?" she asked.

The boy sipped a spoonful of broth, glanced up and flushed. "Just clothes and a bit of food for Jacko the donkey and myself."

"And you speak English?" Shelley pressed.

"Do I?" Pars appeared confused.

Shelley frowned and moved a step closer to the saddlebag. When she did her earrings suddenly began to hum. "What else have you got with you, Pars?" she asked.

Pars appeared nervous. "It's working, isn't it?"

"What is?"

"You are all speaking Pure perfectly yet back at the village I couldn't understand you."

"Pure?"

"Our language is called Pure. Didn't you know that?"

"So what must be working, Pars?" she asked.

"Grandma's Egg." He stood up, stepped towards his saddlebag but stopped when Rhett frowned.

"Let him get it," Shelley said. "My earring is active again." She glanced at Loretta. "Can you go and ask Dee anything has happened to her earrings?"

"Sure," Loretta said and slipped away.

"Just do it slowly," Rhett warned. He watched as the boy withdrew a blue metallic object from a side pocket of the backpack and held it in the palm of his hand.

"Grandma called it a magic egg. It was given to her when she was about my age and told that one day strangers would come to our village, strangers with a good heart and kind souls. They would be looking for their home and the magic egg would help."

Magic egg! Shelley glanced at the object. It was the size and shape of a small bird's egg. It worked, too! Her earrings were activated and it was obviously making their languages understandable to each other.

"How long ago did your Grandma get this magic egg?" she asked.

Pars shrugged. "Grandma's been dead three years now and she was pretty old. Fifty years at least."

"Did your parents look after it, too?"

"No, I never knew my father and Grandma didn't trust my mother. She gave it to me only a few months before she died and asked me to show nobody except the strangers who asked for it. I kept it hidden under our hut and, until now, have shown nobody."

"But why now?" Rhett sounded suspicious. "Why didn't you give it to us when we were in your village?"

"When you arrived we were all excited and I never went near Grandma's egg. It was only after I was whipped that I took it out of its hiding place." He looked sheepish.

"Go on, Pars. Nobody here is going to tease you." Shelley smiled at him. "And they did, didn't they?"

Pars nodded. "Boys are not allowed to be different. We have to be brave, aggressive with a spear and like the fights." He glanced at his feet. "I hated them and often went to Grandma's egg for company."

"And it talked to you?"

"Sort of. When I held it in my hand, it warmed up and feelings rushed into my mind. If I was scared it made me feel confident, if I was lonely it sort of sent tunes through my mind. But for ages it didn't work."

"So you got it out after your beating?"

"Yes. It started working when I took it out from under the hut and unwrapped it. I think it liked the sunshine."

Rhett took the egg from the boy and studied it. "The outer skin could be solar panel that recharges in the sunlight."

"It grew really hot and beeped. The sound changed when I pointed it the direction you used when you left the village. I knew you must be the people Grandma spoke of so I loaded Jacko the next morning and left before anybody was awake." Pars looked back at Shelley. "When your wagon wheel marks disappeared the beeps told me when I went the wrong way. It became a hum when I was going the right way.

While Pars was talking Dee arrived with an excited look on her face and seized Shelley's hand.

"They work, Mum," she whispered. "My earrings are humming."

*

Nothing had been said but it was assumed that Pars would stay with them. Over the next three days he proved to be a quiet boy who helped whenever he could. He liked cooking and had a way with animals, so much so that Krass handed over the care of Zarleg to him. In fact, the Clydesdale readily accepted the tiny donkey and his master.

Over the time, though Rhett kept a suspicious eye on Pars, especially when he went near Dee. To his relief, the boy appeared to be more flattered by the attention he received from Irene who fussed over him, Loretta who constantly chatted to him and Sarine who tended to his back wounds. Dee was more interested in Jacko the donkey and one of the few occasions she chatted excitedly with Pars was when he placed a small blanket over Jacko and invited her to have a ride.

Shelley slipped an arm though Rhett's as they watched Dee climb off the donkey's back after one ride and Pars lifted Cowan on for his turn.

"Still suspicious?" she whispered.

Rhett glanced down at her and grinned. "Okay, I know that he's just a boy but in the village he came from the values are different. I don't want Dee to be hurt, that's all."

"She won't be. If anything he's more interested in Irene."

"Oh don't be silly. Irene's at least seven years older than him."

"About the same age difference as he is to Dee."

Rhett nodded. "I'm being sexist, aren't I?"

Shelley smiled. "No; protective and I love you for being so."

Rhett gazed around the grasslands they still travelled through. There was now no track but the wagon moved over the parched grass and solid ground with ease. Krass had found several citrus trees and proclaimed that the large grapefruit type fruit were a valuable source of food. He also uprooted a tussock plant and cut off the tubular roots. When cooked, they tasted like turnips and were also a good supplement to their dwindling food supply. The streams became less frequent and the ones they did cross had only a little water trickling through.

If it weren't for the constant hum from Par's egg and in Shelley and Dee's earrings, he would have declared themselves lost and turned around. He was still worried at the lack of change but kept his concerns to himself.

They turned and headed towards the wagon that Zarleg pulled along at a snail's pace Rhett acknowledged Irene's wave as she hung up some washing on a line across the back of the wagon and turned to see Krass coming up behind them. As usual, the elderly man had gone on a morning's reconnaissance. Perhaps he had found another food source.

His stride, however, was urgent and the pair walked back to meet him.

"What is it?" Rhett asked when Krass arrived looking hot and apprehensive.

'There's a moving dust cloud behind us. I think we're being followed by people on horses. They're moving quite quickly and will overtake us before noon, I'd say."

"Villagers from Par's village?"

Krass frowned as he tugged on his beard. "No, they only had working horses and donkeys like Pars' who would not be stirring up the dust like these ones. These are mounts being ridden almost at a gallop."

"So what do you suggest?" Shelley whispered.

"I found another stream ahead that winds out of a small gully. If we can get there you can all hide while I go ahead with Zarleg and the wagon. If they only find me they may go away."

"They won't," Shelley said. "They want either Pars or us, probably all of us. They know we're here and have some way of tracing us."

"You mean something like Par's egg?"

Shelley nodded. "Or my earrings."

"We can't outrun them," Krass said.

"So the stream is our only hope," Rhett argued.

"And the first place they'd search."

"What then?" Rhett felt annoyed.

"Let's get everyone into the wagon and I want to talk to Pars about the egg."

*

The stream twisted through gravel, the water was only knee deep in the deepest part and the clay banks sloped up at an easy angle. Krass led Zarleg and the wagon up the far bank and nodded back at the wheel marks leading up the far side. He next took the Clydesdale up onto the dry grass, walked in a tight circle and brought the wagon back to the centre of the stream. From there, he turned downstream away from the gully and into a small gravel island that the stream flowed around.

"I hope it works," he grumbled for the wagon, though in a dip, stuck out like a sailing ship with the canvas blowing in the breeze. He walked back to the wheel marks and used a brush to wipe out the hoof prints from Zarleg's return journey. A moment later he stood back and studied his handy work.

"Looks okay," Rhett said. "I doubt if anyone will know we came back down the far side.

"Yeah," the old man whispered. "Let's hope Pars is right and his egg does what he said it would."

"I'll tie Jacko to the farthest side." Pars said when they reached the wagon. He led the donkey around and tied him to the backboard. "Sit fellow," he instructed and patted his neck. "Now don't move."

Rhett glanced up and saw Loretta follow the children and women into the wagon. As she closed the canvas cover, the two horses, wagon and everything within sort of vibrated, faded and disappeared.

"So it did work," Krass muttered.

"Shelley thought it might. As long as there is no sudden movement inside or anyone goes too close, we will remain invisible."

"And if they have a tracking device?"

Shelley came running along the far bank. She glanced at the stones, jumped from one dry one to another so no footprints were left and rushed up.

"Come on," she gasped. "The dust cloud is getting close."

"And you hid your earrings?" he asked as they headed for the spot where they knew the wagon was.

Shelley placed her hands on her empty earlobes. "No I just dropped them on the ground a hundred metres out. If anyone has a tracer and finds them it'll look as if they were accidentally dropped." She screwed her nose up. "We'll, I hope that's what it'll look like. I made a cross reference to some trees so I know where to go back to afterwards if I need to recover them."

"And Dee's?" The wagon appeared as they passed through the shield.

For a moment Shelley never replied as they scrambled aboard and squeezed inside. She turned to Dee. "Can you still do it?"

Dee grabbed her hand. "Sure Mum. I just asked it to switch the tracer off and it did."

"And how did you know it would do that?" Rhett sat down and pulled the canvas flap aside. From the inside looking out, nothing appeared any different.

Dee shrugged. "I didn't," she said. "Pars suggested I try and the humming stopped."

"If it's like my egg it will sense her fear and protect her," Pars whispered from across the wagon.

"They're coming!" Krass hissed. "Don't talk or move."

Rhett stared out but was not expecting the sound that reached his ears. Instead of the galloping horses he heard a faint whine of an engine, almost like that of a modern jet airliner coming down to an airport. Shelley's hand squeezed his arm and he caught her frightened eyes.

Nobody in the wagon moved but all eyes were out the front through the flap that Rhett had pulled back. Zarleg twitched his ears and Rhett hoped that the horse would not make a sound or stamp his foot, something he often did if he was stubborn or annoyed.

Krass slipped lightly to the ground and stepped forward to wrap an arm around the horse's neck. "Hush, boy," he soothed and remained beside him.

Zarleg appeared to sense what was required for, apart from swishing his tail slightly, he remained still.

The whine became a roar and without further warning, a gigantic vehicle the size of a truck arrived. It had no wheels and floated on a balloon type base. Rhett's heart pounded. It was a hovercraft painted a camouflaged grey and khaki. Worse, though was the black swastika painted on the bonnet below the windscreen and German language words along the fuselage.

The vehicle moved slowly down to the stream and stopped where the wagon wheel tracks led up the far bank. The left front doors opened and a man in grey uniform stepped out. He lifted his peaked cap and wiped his brow as he turned.

"Oh no," Shelley gasped in a petrified whisper. "But how? The tsintaosaurus killed and ate him."

Rhett also felt cold ice grip his back. The hovercraft driver was Dedrik Jaeger.

*

The rear hovercraft door opened and a boy was shoved out by a storm trooper dressed in an old-fashioned Nazi World War Two uniform and square helmet. The boy fell to the ground, glanced up and fended off a kick as he staggered to his feet. Blood poured down the side of his face as he turned and stared almost directly at them.

"It's Flanz," Pars gasped. "What have they done to him?"

He went to stand up but was seized from behind by Krass. "Don't move, Lad," the old man hissed. "If they..."

Pars fought his emotions and remained seated with his face white and intense. Assured that the boy wouldn't do anything rash, Rhett turned his attention back to the hovercraft.

Some sort of argument was going on. He could hear shouting but couldn't make out the words as Jaeger grabbed Flanz by the collar and shook him. Two more storm troopers appeared and fanned out in defensive positions along the stream. One used a pair of binoculars to study the terrain. As he turned slowly around, Rhett clenched his teeth and felt Shelley's fingernails cut into his upper arm.

If they were seen...

The man hesitated when he faced their direction but continued his surveillance beyond them and across the far bank. So they were completely invisible! Rhett relaxed a little and gave Dee beside him, a reassuring nod.

The arguing continued with the obviously annoyed Jaeger venting his anger on the boy, who turned, screamed back and pointed downstream in their direction.

"He can see us!" Shelley gasped.

"But the others can't," Rhett replied.

Flanz reacted. He lashed out with a fist, caught Jaeger unaware and sent him reeling onto the ground. The boy seized his opportunity and ran... straight down the stream bank towards them.

"Help me!" His hysterical words cut the air like a knife,

He slipped, rose again and succeeded in getting fifty metres along the bank before Jaeger rose to his feet, stood with his legs apart and drew a sidearm from a holster.

"No!" Pars gasped.

The Nazi raised the weapon and fired twice. Two popping sounds rang through the air, Flanz screamed, flung his arms out and pitched forward into the water. A circle of current turned dark red with blood before it floated away. Little could be seen now except for a brief view of his upper torso and head lying face down in the bloodstained water.

Jaeger barked a command, the storm troopers all climbed aboard the hovercraft, there was a roar and the vehicle moved forward into the stream. Water beneath it churned and frothed. Rhett had another terrible moment of anxiety as it appeared to come their way but instead, the hovercraft forded the stream and rose up the far bank to the plateau above.

The engine revved and dust replaced water fanning out underneath as the vehicle began to accelerate forward and out of sight,

Fifty metres ahead there was an explosion, so loud that Rhett's ears rung. He grabbed Shelley and Dee and just held onto them as an orange ball of flame and black smoke spiralled into the air. Huge chunks of metal spun up with whistling sounds of secondary explosions and high curves of tracer bullets accompanying them. A blast of hot putrid smoke descended and everyone erupted in coughing spasms.

"Stay here!" Rhett gasped.

He jumped down and ran forward in a crouch along the bank. He threw himself on the bank and crawled over short grass up the embankment. Something touched him and he leaped in sheer fright. He turned. Shelley was crawling up the bank beside him.

"I told you to stay back," he hissed but really felt relieved to have her with him.

"And leave you alone to cope?" Her lips were in a determined line as she wriggled in beside him and they moved up until the scene before them unfolded.

The hovercraft was a ball of towering flames with ammunition still exploding and lines of vapour vibrating up into the black smoke above. Only one blackened body lay motionless on the ground twenty metres in front of the fire.

"Nobody would have escaped that," Rhett muttered.

Shelley nodded and stood up. Rhett went to pull her back but saw the strange expression in her eyes. He stood beside her and they both covered their faces to protect themselves from the intense heat.

"What are you doing?" he asked as she walked parallel to the burning vehicle with her eyes focused in a different direction. "Come back, Shelley. You can't do anything to help."

Shelley ignored him and continued to walk through the grass. She stopped, turned and pointed to a rock beyond the remains of the hovercraft.

"I was right," she said.

"Right?"

Shelley turned and stared at him. "I know what happened," she said.

"What?"

"That hovercraft blew up when it was right above my earring there. Remember, I told you I had taken a couple of reference points so I could find them again, if necessary. I believe my earring worked like a land mine and exploded when they drove by."

"But why?"

"To protect us," Shelley whispered. "Some sophisticated device knew we were in trouble, perhaps it was activated by the terror in my mind."

"But if you were wearing them..."

'The ultimate military defence if a combatant is about to be tortured or who is already dead. Oh no!" Shelley stood up and streaked back to the wagon, which was now visible with the people and animals standing beside it.

Shelley tore up and grabbed Dee. "Your earrings," she screamed. "Take them off."

"What is it Mum?" Dee howled but reached up and unscrewed them. She handed the pair to Shelley who tore up the bank and threw them as far as she could over the water.

Rhett expected to see a ripple as the tiny objects hit the water. Instead, there was an almighty bang, two violent water sprouts rose in the air, fanned out and dropped back like a gigantic waterfall. The spray drenched Shelley and himself as he grabbed her in his arms.

"Dee would have been as terrified as I was," she sobbed. "If my ones were activated, I thought... Oh Rhett, if she was still wearing them she would have all been killed like those in the hovercraft."

"Mum!" Dee screamed. "Mum!" She tore into Shelley's arms and sobbed incoherently as the others arrived to help.

*

CHAPTER FIFTEEN

Shelley stared around at the confusion as everyone absorbed what had happened. The wagon and animals were still sitting undamaged but visible on the shingle bank, the hovercraft had stopped exploding but was burning furiously as was a circle of grass around it and Flanz's body floated between two rocks in the stream. His blood had floated away and no more appeared from the lifeless corpse.

"Come on everyone," she said. "We have to move?"

"But why?" Loretta asked.

"I doubt if this hovercraft is the only one. More could follow." Shelley turned and waved her hand out over the plains. "Anybody could have come through a portal and be heading this way."

"I'll check back." Krass glanced at Pars. "Can I borrow Jacko, Lad?"

"Sure," the boy muttered without much interested. He stared along at his dead friend. "He never hurt anyone, you know. It was all talk. He didn't deserve this."

Shelley walked across and placed an arm around him. "We can do nothing for him now, Pars," she said. "But you can be proud."

Pars stared down at her. "Me. What did I do?"

"Saved our lives. Without your grandmother's egg we would have all been shot as ruthlessly as Flanz."

"I guess but it didn't help him, did it? Not like your earrings that blew the bastards up."

"Your egg activated my earrings, you know."

Pars nodded slightly and tears rolled down his face. He wiggled away from Shelley, ran away, splashed through the water to the nearside bank and ran along away from everything. She was about to follow but Rhett caught her arm.

"Let him go," he whispered. "Boys don't like to be seen crying."

"That's stupid," howled Dee. She waded the stream, ran after Pars and waited beside him as he stood on the bank looking down at the body.

"Let's get the wagon up the far bank and ready to leave," Rhett said.

Shelley nodded. "We need to bury Flanz."

It took a while to dig graves for the stony ground was too difficult to use. They finally resorted to digging into a clay bank and rolling out the stones in their way. Flanz and also the other body, the stormtrooper who had been thrown from the hovercraft were dragged across and buried. Sarine said a remembrance elegy and Pars told about a couple of things that Flanz and himself had got up to back in the village. It brought smiles through the tears.

In contrast, there was grim silence as soil and stones were placed over the stormtrooper's body. He was also only a youth.

"He never asked to be killed in an alien world, either," Shelley whispered. "We don't even know his name."

*

The fire had died out but the white-hot hovercraft hulk was just that, an empty metal shell with everything inside incinerated. The fierce heat had devoured every trace of Dedrik Jaeger and the other stormtroopers.

"Of course, he may have more clones?" Loretta whispered as the women stood at the edge of the burnt grass a few moments after the funerals.

Shelley turned and frowned. "And you think that was what he was?"

"Of course. We had the knowledge to do it." She stared at Shelley. "I wouldn't be surprised if you aren't one."

"Me?"

"Of course. Your identity arrived on Rhett's world with your physical blueprints intact and made a duplicate body for you."

"We could be clones, too," Irene added.

"The difference between us and this Jaeger is that our society uses our knowledge to help us survive, not to offer immortality to ruthless militants," Sarine said.

Shelley stared at her friend. "And you know about this practice?"

"I had heard that the girifa had succeeded in making several physical bodies for their leaders. On course, only one could contain the identity of the actual person. The others were either kept in reserve or were lived in by others as doubles to mislead any enemy. Jaeger's army could have done the same." Sarine flashed her brown eyes at Shelley. "Surely, you'd know something about this."

"Except for isolated events that come to me, I have no memories of my life before meeting Rhett."

"Of course," Sarine replied. "I'm sorry."

"No, it's okay. I have a feeling I don't want to remember most of my life." Shelley glanced at Dee still with Pars. "I miss knowledge of my children as they grew up, of course."

She turned and walked back to where Rhett was tying down the canvas on the wagon after checking the gear inside. He glanced up as Shelley approached.

"Did you see Krass?" he asked

Shelley glanced at her watch. "No. It's over an hour."

"I know. We need to leave soon. I hope he isn't too long."

Ten minutes later, an almost galloping Jacko appeared in the distance surround by a cloud of dust. As soon as the donkey arrived,

Krass slipped off with an agitated look on his face.

"We need to move," he gasped. "There's dust right across the plains to the foothills. At a guess I'd say there's an whole army coming our way from out there."

"But what way should we go?" Shelley asked.

"Ahead. Follow your beeper."

"I haven't got my earrings any more."

Krass glowered and turned to Pars. "And your egg?"

"I haven't tried," the boy admitted. He took the object from his pocket, gasped and, without saying any reason why, threw it as hard as he could along the stream.

"What'd you do that for?" Krass muttered angrily.

"It was burning hot," Pars gasped. "If it explodes like Shelley and Dee's earrings..."

Shelley turned and caught the tiny object in her eye as it dropped like a stone towards the water. She braced herself waiting for an explosion ... but none came!

Instead, a cloud of steam rose where the egg had hit the water. It grew thicker and higher until one whole area of the river was covered. But there was no sound, not even hiss that steam would normally emit. The water still in view was not affected either but just flowed on through the rocks.

Slowly the cloud spiralled in on itself, became denser and flattened itself into a five metre round white marble boulder so solid, Shelley felt as if she could climb on it. The smoke appearance disappeared and for a moment this glistening solid object filled the stream from bank to bank. It wasn't an illusion either for the water stopped flowing and banked up until two mini waterfalls tumbled down from each side and continued the journey downstream.

The movement did not stop. For the first time, noise filled the air. A faint grinding turned to a loud cracking sound, four massive cracks fanned out from the central base of the boulder and it split open like a shell being peeled from a hard-boiled egg.

Bits splashed into the water and the stream reverted to its original course. However, straddling the entire stream was a wooden portal door five times as big as any other they had used. The view of the stream inside faded even though the water still flowed beneath. In its place was a long metallic corridor lit up by recessed white lights.

"It worked, Pars," Shelley gasped. "A portal has opened for us."

"And big enough to drive the wagon through." Rhett turned to Krass. "Can you bring the wagon down?'

But Krass had already disappeared up the bank and Shelley could hear him giving brisk commands to Zarleg. Meanwhile, Pars had reached Jacko and the women had gathered Corwin and Dee up in their care.

"We're ready," Loretta called.

"Wait for Krass and the wagon," Shelley said. "We'll all go in together. I don't want anybody left behind."

She started! Above the sound of gurgling water she could hear the far off sound of vehicle engines, seemingly hundreds of them... They were growing louder by the second.

The Clydesdale seemed to be just ambling back down the far bank with the wagon behind and the old man perched in the driver's seat.

"Hurry. Krass!" she screamed.

*

Krass arrived with Zarleg and the wagon, everyone clamoured aboard with Pars at the back where he tied Jacko's lead to the backboard.

"We're ready," he shouted.

Shelley sat beside him and stared out as Krass issued commands for Zarleg to start forward. The horse, though, snorted and refused to walk into the stream and on through the portal.

"Do something!" Dee who had taken a place beside Krass, howled.

"Come on, Old Fellow; in two worlds you have not let me down. Just walk into the tunnel you see."

Zarleg snorted, stamped his foot but refused to move.

Shelley watched in horror as her daughter jumped off the buckboard and landed on all fours in the stream. She staggered up, soaking wet and waded forward to the horse where she patted his nose and grabbed the reins in her hands.

Krass let the reins go and Dee soothed Zarleg as she stepped forward towards the portal.

"Come on, Zarleg," she said. "Come inside and there'll be an extra bag of oats for you tonight."

Whether the horse understood or not, Shelley didn't know but the horse whinnied and stepped forward. The wagon creaked and bumped along the stream, water flowed almost to Zarleg's knees, the wagon wheels and Dee's waist but they moved slowly forward. Dee reached the portal and stepped inside. Her feet and soaked dress appeared as she continued to talk to the horse.

It was a strange sight for she was out of the water but level, not above it. It was as if a glass barrier was across the front to stop the water from flowing back inside. Zarleg snorted but continued on. When his forelegs hit the dry portal floor, he seemed to sense it was dry and quickened his pace.

Shelley turned and looked out the rear, She screamed for a roar of an engine filled her ears. A brown camouflaged military transporter on six massive tyres appeared upstream at the ford. It plunged forward with its wheels churning water everywhere and the vertical exhaust shouting out a cloud of steam. It stopped midstream.

"Hurry!" Shelley screamed.

The transporter turned to face them, a top hatch opened and another peak-capped officer stood up. He barked an order and the vehicle headed in their direction. Shelley stared terrified as a stormtrooper appeared out of a lower hatch, held up a machine gun and fired.

The aim was too high but the noise of the discharges and whistling bullets provided that little extra motivation for Zarleg. He snorted and broke into a gallop that would have pulled Dee over if she hadn't let the reins go. The horse thundered forward, the creaking groaning wagon came next and the scared donkey galloped up the rear.

Shelley saw Dee sitting on the floor as they tore by. Her daughter leaped to her feet and shrank back, just as Jacko actually jumped over her.

Gradually, Zarleg slowed and came to a stop, snorting and frothing at the mouth. Dee ran forward but was grabbed by Krass who had jumped down beside her.

"No," he shouted. "If Zarleg kicks you..."

Dee stopped and stood shaking in the old man's arms.

But the portal had not closed!

The hovercraft had arrived and followed them in!

It roared and moved forward. The lower hatch had closed but the officer still stood at the top hatch staring at them with an expression of glee on his face.

Shelley gasped for it was Dedrik Jaeger again. He actually focused on her eyes, brought a pistol out and raised it.

In that same instant a bubble dropped from the ceiling over the vehicle, there was a howl of escaping air and Jaeger, followed by three crew members were sucked backwards out the rear of the portal, which closed and disappeared. The last Shelley saw of Jaeger was his face that had turned to a contorted silent scream of terror. His eyes bulged and cheeks sagged as if he was deprived of oxygen.

"Oh my stars," Shelley gasped and grabbed for Pars who was still beside her.

The portal and the stormtroopers had gone. Instead, the corridor curved away out of sight in the distance. The transporter had stalled, ominous and silent behind Jacko, the wagon and everyone inside.

"Dee?" Shelley screamed.

"I'm here, Mum." Dee moved into sight. She was drenched and shivering but stood grinning at her.

"You stay here," Rhett ordered. He jumped down and followed by Krass walked cautiously back to the transporter.

The men walked behind it, appeared over the rear top and Krass disappeared down the hatch the crew had been sucked out of. He returned a moment later, spoke to Rhett and have Shelley a thumbs-up sign.

"They've all gone," Pars gasped.

"Yes," Shelley replied grimly for her heart was still racing. "Nice of them to leave a modern vehicle for us to use."

*

The transporter was empty and offered no real clues as to how it came to be in this world. It smelt of oil and sweaty bodies with food scraps and litter around that showed it had been travelled in for several hours. The only clues were two personal instruments that could have been communication devices. Rhett could get neither to work and turned his attention to the dashboard. The numbers on the controls showed digits he understood and appeared to be calibrated in kilometres while the levers and foot pedals appeared to be similar to an automatic vehicle at home. Two monitors were off but the one that remained on showed a map.

"Look at this, Krass," he said.

"Don't know this new mechanical stuff much," the old man muttered and stared at the screen. "Looks like a map of a road, though." He pointed to the screen. "Those side lines must be the walls of this tunnel. Doesn't show much else."

Rhett rubbed his chin in thought and touched a green diamond at the bottom of the screen. It immediately became larger. When he moved his finger to the left and the map became smaller. He continued and a scale of numbers appeared along the base.

"Metres, I'd say," he muttered and continued to zoom outwards until the road was just a ribbon. "Oh hell!" The road went around on a circle and that was it. There were no side roads or any other items like contour lines, symbols indicating buildings or natural features, just a black circle showing the road with grey lines on each side.

Rhett touched several of the other diamond shaped controls but, except for changing the screens colour and superimposing grid lines, they offered no other explanation. The grid was divided into hundred-metre squares. It only took a brief calculation to realise the circular road was exactly two kilometres long.

"Aye, what's keeping you?" Shelley's head popped in the opened hatch above.

Rhett glanced up and grinned. "Come and look at this."

"Place stinks of too many bodies," she replied as she swung in and climbed over to plonk in the driver's seat. She glanced around. "Looks like a typical reconnaissance vehicle that armies use. Hydrogen extraction motor, solar energy electronics and..."

"You know about these vehicles?"

"Of course, they're common..." Shelley gulped and stared at

Rhett. "They aren't are they?"

"Not where I came from. Can you remember anything else?"

Shelley frowned and shook her head. "No, this vehicle seems familiar, that's all."

"And the language?"

Shelley frowned. "I can't read it. Looks like German, you know, long words with lots of 'ks',"

"Look at the monitor map, Shelley."

She studied it, fiddled the controls like Rhett had done and stared at him. Pouting, she reached up to another monitor and a blast of static filled the cab. "No radio or visual contact with any base," she said. "We're definitely in a new world."

"But is it?" Rhett asked.

"The road, you mean?"

"Yes, it's perfectly round, exactly two kilometres in circumference and has no other physical features showing."

" I think I know," Shelley whispered.

"We're underground?" Krass replied.

"No, the opposite. I think we're inside a gigantic spaceship. Remember that message from Rear Admiral Medina?"

"Your older self?"

Shelley nodded.

"And you're sure we're in a spacecraft?"

"Not certain but it seems that way. Perhaps Loretta, Irene or Sarine can help." She reached forward, pressed a pad and everything turned off. "If the engine or electronics are still running they could affect the oxygen content in the air. We should leave it here and use Zarleg and the wagon for transport." She shrugged. "With the circular road, there's not a huge distance to travel, anyway."

They found little else of interest so the three climbed out of the transporter and headed back to the wagon. As they did so Rhett found himself gasping for breath. The air smelt of cut grass. He reached out, found Shelley's hand and dropped to the floor.

*

Shelley awoke with a start. Oh no, it was happening again. She was somewhere new and in a bed under clean sheets with no clothes on. Rhett was beside her also without any clothes on. Their clothes were arranged in two neat piles on a side bench. The air smelt warm and a tint of grass filled tickled her sense buds. Of course, that was the smell she'd noticed just before... She frowned. Before what? Memory of the corridor, transporter and wagon flooded back... but where were the others.

Perhaps she was dreaming! No she was definitely awake.

The room had no windows but lighting came from the walls and ceilings. She turned and noticed more beds lined up in what appeared to be a dormitory. Everyone was, asleep beneath white sheets and with their clothes in neat piles beside them. The women were on the left side and the men to the right.

"Rhett," she whispered and gently shook his arm, He sighed but didn't awaken. She hastily pulled on her jeans and top before walking over to the children. They were asleep couldn't be awoken and nor could anybody else. Everyone appeared peaceful with steadily rising and falling chests, closed eyes and slight smiles on their lips. On closer inspection she noticed that their pupils beneath the lids moved. So they were all dreaming? By the facial expressions the dreams were pleasant ones.

An end door slid open as she approached and she walked out into a bathroom with western style toilets, showers, baths and sinks arranged in alcoves behind sliding metal doors. To the left was another door that led to a living quarters with a kitchen on the left and couches to the right. Shelley frowned. The room contained no electronic equipment such as televisions or computers. Nor were there any other items one might find in a human home such as newspapers, books or magazines. The walls were bare with or art, calendars or clocks on them. She glanced at her wrist and found she was still wearing her watch. Three days had gone by since she had last looked at it. The time was 0620 hours, still early morning... or it was in the world they had moved from.

She turned on a shower and found the water was quite hot. That was different. Didn't spaceships use vacuum gasses to cleanse the body so water would be saved? She blinked. How did she know that? She promised herself a warm shower as soon as possible and continued her exploration.

At the far end of the living quarters was a larger door. It slid open when she approached to reveal a field of grass. The grass was real but nothing else was. She stood in a circular grassed area as large as a football field and surrounded by an opaque glass that reached up above her to the underside of a dome. Both the unhitched wagon and the transporter stood parked beside a barn-like building with a wooden front door and open loft window above it.

Shelley turned and assured herself the door she'd just walked through was still there. It was! She tested it by walking back inside, saw no change so went back 'outside' and into the barn. She sighed in relief. Both Zarleg with Jacko were lying unconscious beside each other on a pile of straw. Both animals looked as if they'd been well looked after as there were both water and troughs of food along one wall.

A feeling of apprehension rather than worry filled her mind as she summed the situation up. On the positive side, everyone was alive and physically in good condition, the air was fresh and clean clothes and food were awaiting everyone. It was logical, therefore that her family and friends would awaken at some time. However, the negatives were strong. Why were they inside what she assumed was a spaceship? Who held the power to render them all asleep and exert complete control over them? Lastly, why was she the only one awake?

She was about to walk out of the barn when a woman appeared by the open door. She was tall, slim and dressed in a silver military uniform.

"Welcome to the reconstituted Battlecruiser Sif, Shelley Medina," she said in a soft voice. "My name is Isis, who in ancient mythology from Rhett's Earth was the goddess of rebirth. You were awoken before your companions as we have much to discuss and fail safe procedures need to be overridden."

Isis stepped closer until she stood within two metres of Shelley. Her skin was tanned and blonde shoulder length hair, shiny. In some ways she looked too perfect.

Shelley frowned and stared into the stranger's eyes. Again, though perfect, they looked different. Deep within the black pupils, she was sure she could see a dull oval like a camera lens.

"You are not human or even and identity in a cloned body," she gasped. "What are you?"

The woman smiled. "You are very perceptive, Shelley. Most humans, or indeed girifa would take hours, if not days to realise we are not biologically alive. I am an android created in the same manner as this spaceship itself from the so-called 'black box' that survived the destruction of the original Sif.

My aim, and I hope still yours, is to right the wrongs that have been created in conflicting universes over the last century of linear time." She placed her opened hands and arms out. "Your family and friends are safe and will awaken when it is deemed the proper time. Come through to the bridge that was once your ancestor's command centre. I assume you know of the rear admiral who inherited your name?"

"My ancestor? Don't you mean my older self or my descendent?"

"No, she was neither. In linear time she lived almost a century before you. She was your great grandmother but her genes survived through to your daughter and yourself. Any memories you may have received from her were inherited and genetically enhanced because of their importance to the situation we are now in."

"Which is?"

"That is what I am about to explain." Isis smiled and turned back to the barn door. "Please follow me."

*

CHAPTER SIXTEEN

The room Shelley entered was a control centre with screens, keyboards and other electronic equipment everywhere. There was a hum of air-conditioning and a smell of polish filled the air. She suspected that the smell was artificially made but made no comment.

"Take a seat." Isis extended her hand to a large sofa that faced a gigantic screen. "Coffee?"

"No thank you."

Isis snapped her fingers and the screen ahead lit up to show a star-studded universe. "Rear Admiral Medina and the Battlecruiser Sif were destroyed within minutes of entering their final battle. The scene before you is time enhanced to show you the aftermath of this battle."

"But you said we were on the Sif," Shelley said.

"The reconstituted Sif," Isis corrected. "When the original Sif was destroyed the enemy was very thorough. Every piece of debris was vaporised but even the girifas' advanced technology was inferior to our own. The 'black box' I mentioned earlier was, in fact a nanocraft, smaller than a grain of dust. Inside, my ancestors I guess you'd call them, were microscopic androids capable of reproducing. This they did. It took ninety-three earth years to get to the stage we are now at. The video you are about to see contracts that time to fifteen minutes."

Shelley watched, fascinated as the stars changed into a blur and a planet appeared below. "Rhett's Earth!" she gasped.

"Yes, but in the eighteenth century when it was even more primitive than in Rhett's time. There were no electronics at all and was a perfect place for us. A simple cloning system hid us from the telescopes that probed the skies in the more enlightened countries."

A silver construction began to emerge. From a central sphere, beams fanned out like eight bicycle spokes. Once uniform in length, a circular outer construction joined them until the shape was like that bicycle wheel without any tyre added. Once formed, the interior triangular sections were filled in with spider web efficiency until a gigantic domed spaceship orbited the Earth below. The number fifty flashed up and the scene changed to the inside.

"That took the nanoandroids fifty years," Isis explained.

"The interior view showed everything being constructed from complicated electronics to the crew quarters with artificial gravity created by a central spinning cylinder. Vegetation began to grow in domes like the one Shelley had just come from. Everything for human habitation was created and finally the scene showed a row of twenty or more transparent cocoon shaped objects with human females asleep inside. One awoke and climbed out, dressed from clothes on a nearby bench and turned. It was Isis!

"That is the present situation." Isis turned the monitor off and faced Shelley. "I am an android with a biological skin and body features. I do not, however, need food or air to operate. Nano-electronics power me. Human features such as higher traits of conscience and empathy actually come from Rear Admiral Medina's own mind." Isis smiled. "In that way, I could actually be your relation."

"And the reason for all of this?" Shelley asked.

"To continue the rear admiral's original orders. The real enemy was not the girifa but the humans on Earth and the philosophy that was not destroyed in the mid-twentieth century."

"The Nazis of World War Two?"

"Exactly."

"So why don't you just go and do it? Your advanced technology should be capable of destroying them and their whole alternative Earth in an instant."

Isis nodded. "Two reasons. One is that Gavin's Earth is the alternate one while the one of Dedrik Jaeger and his clones is the original. After any future universe amalgamation, his world will be the survivor, not yours or Gavin's."

"So back to my original question."

"Your ancestor and her colleagues were highly principled. When artificial intelligence and reproducing life forms were created, fail-safe procedures were included that, even with our own advanced knowledge, we cannot override. We can advise and help but we cannot destroy any civilisation, even one as abhorrent as the Nazis."

"So we're here to do your dirty work?"

"That's a crude way of putting it. Your ancestor had genetically enhanced genes that were passed onto her eldest female child who continued the process. You inherited them as Dee does from you."

"And what do these genes do?"

"Mainly allow memories and knowledge to be retained. Normally when someone dies, their memories and everything they learned, good or bad, dies with them. You still have your mother's and grandmother's memories deep inside your mind."

"Why just my mother and grandmother?"

"Historically in most species, males are responsible for ninety percent of the crime and wars. She was a broadminded woman but still had her prejudices. She did not trust the half of the human population known as males. Many advanced civilisations have also over reacted, shall we say, to this. One has no males at all and historical frozen sperm is used for reproduction."

Shelley screwed he nose up. "How awful."

"Possibly but they are a very peaceful civilisation."

"But little better than the Nazis with their genocide of people they didn't like."

"An interesting comparison, Shelley. I see you are your own

person and not just a reproduction of the rear admiral."

"I am," Shelley replied. "Now, before we continue, I'd like Rhett to be awoken so he can see what I've just viewed and be able to help with any future decisions I'll need to make."

Isis studied her. "And not make any decision for you?"

"No, Rhett is not like that. We are a team who work together as one. We love each other!" Shelley swallowed her anger and made her loud voice quieter. "Is that an emotion you don't understand?"

"I'm learning," Isis whispered. "We can learn these human traits, you know. The fail-safe only overrides emotions that hinder the advancement of life... biological or electronic."

"And you're alive?" Shelley spat.

"I like to think so," Isis replied.

Shelley felt her face heat up in embarrassment. "I'm sorry," she said. "I did not mean to hurt your feelings."

"So you accept that I have them?"

"Obviously," Shelley whispered. "And thank you. Without your help we wouldn't be here safe and out of Dedrik Jaeger's clutches."

"Yes, he's a perfect example of advanced technology gone wrong. We have traced six of his clones. The original Jaeger died twenty years ago."

"So you will let Gavin awaken?"

"Is that an order?"

"No it's a request."

"Shelley, I am beginning to like you." Isis stood up. "Come along, we can be there when Rhett awakens and you can introduce me." She smiled. "Isn't that what humans do?"

*

CHAPTER SEVENTEEN

Even with their sophisticated surveillance systems and modern weaponry, Rhett was worried. At the back of his mind, too was an argument he'd had with Shelley. She had insisted on coming but after his opinion that she should remain with Dee and Corwin was backed by the others she had reluctantly agreed to remain behind.

Dressed in authentic Nazi uniforms of the era, he was the vehicle's driver. Krass was a German general sitting beside him and Pars, the gunnery officer stood in the open turret behind them. Again in keeping with the armies of the time, none of the women were included. However, Loretta and Irene accompanied them as identities as they drove through the portal in the Nazi transporter. The road ahead hugged the mountainside where low clouds hung over the mountains and the temperature hovered only a few degrees above freezing.

According to Isis's research, they would arrive at their destination in April 1943. The road ahead wound up a Norwegian fiord to the underground atomic research station where seven atomic bombs were ready to be placed in submarines for transportation to the port of St Nazaire in coastal France. From there, two bombs were to be taken by submarine and exploded off New York and Halifax, Canada in suicide missions. Five others were being delivered to a nearby Luftwaffe base and loaded onto especially adapted Heinkel He177 bombers with destinations of London and Manchester in England. Two more bombers would fly east to advanced bases in occupied Poland for refuelling and ultimately drop bombs over Moscow and Leningrad.

"We'll send back reports of everything we see."

Loretta's words boomed out in Rhett's mind and he watched the two almost invisible identities fly out the hatchway. Loretta flew ahead while Irene circled back to survey the road behind where the portal shimmied and disappeared. They were alone until it opened for their return journey.

"I don't like it," Krass grumbled. "Too damned quiet, if you ask me."

"According to Isis there is a major check point fifteen kilometres behind us. Any vehicle this far along would be automatically regarded as friendly."

Krass stared at Rhett. "One telephone call back and they'll know we never went through that check point."

"Not if Irene burns out the lines with her electrical charge. The radios have also been electronically blocked."

"So they'll be suspicious."

Rhett shrugged. Everything Krass said was true. Whatever the risk though, they were now committed.

"The tunnel entrance is a kilometre ahead. There is a guardhouse with a barrier across the road," Loretta reported.

"The road behind is deserted and I am about to short circuit the telephone lines. Two submarines are coming up the fiord and appear to be heading for that cave mouth we have on our maps," Irene added. *"Do you want me to look closer?"*

"No, just get those telephone lines out." Rhett knew his silent words would reach Irene.

"Right, Rhett."

Irene went silent but Loretta continued to give details of the guards and other personnel at the tunnel. She confirmed that the road continued deep inside the mountain and spiralled down to an underground chamber where a wharf had been constructed that was capable of docking several U-boats, the name the Nazis called their submarines.

"There are troops and vehicles everywhere, here," Loretta reported. *"A railway line leads further back into the mountain. I think Isis's maps are spot on. I can't see any bombs here, though. They mustn't have arrived yet."*

"Good. Now come back. We don't want you to get lost." Rhett said.

Loretta's laugh was nervous. *"I'm okay. There are floodlights everywhere. I'm just hovering up between them."*

"Don't you take any risks, Girl," Krass muttered. *"You are too valuable."*

"Am I?"

Rhett caught Krass's eyes and saw the concern in the his eyes. Now clean-shaven and in the immaculate uniform he looked years younger than the guy he'd first met.

"Okay," Krass muttered. "I'm allowed to be worried about her."

"Of course," Rhett whispered as he swung the steering wheel to navigate an eighty-degree corner.

"I see the guardhouse," Pars called from behind.

"Come down." Rhett replied. "I doubt if a soldier would be manning a machine gun this far in."

Pars dropped down and closed the hatch. He turned and his face appeared white in the dim light. He looked scared!

"Don't talk unless you have to," Rhett said. "But if you need to, just relax. Your voice and accent will be in the perfect 20th century German we are now speaking."

"I know," Pars said. "I hope I don't let everyone down, that's all."

"You'll be fine, Son," Krass replied. "Irene will be proud of you."

The old man winked at Rhett. Perhaps he knew something about the pair Rhett had not cottoned onto.

But more important things now occupied his mind. He slowed as their vehicle approached the red and white barrier lowered across the road. Two guards in grey uniform and holding sub-machine guns stood at full alert beside the guardhouse to their right.

He slowed and stopped before the barrier, wound down his window and waited as one guard approached.

"General von Rothstein has arrived to inspect the loading of the packages." Rhett hoped that Isis's transference of fictitious details into ancient Nazi records would work.

The sergeant frowned and glanced at a clipboard in his hand. He turned his eyes into the cab and ignored Rhett. "You are not expected until tomorrow, General von Rothstein," he stated. "I must check with my superiors."

"Of course, Sergeant," Krass replied in a surprisingly authoritative voice. "You would not be doing your duty if you didn't verify our arrival."

The sergeant saluted and retreated into the guardhouse but Rhett noticed the second guard still stood by the barrier with the machine gun in his hand. There was nothing slack about them.

The guard returned with a frown on his face. "The telephone line is out." He hesitated for the first time. "British bombers flew up the fiord over night and we heard explosions. They could have bombed the lines."

"That is a distinct possibility," Krass replied. "We passed a hillside where there were a couple of bomb craters." He laughed. "If that is all the damage the British can do, we have little to fear."

"No General von Rothstein." The guard remained serious. "Your identification papers please, Sir."

Krass handed a leather bound booklet to Rhett who handed it onto the guard. The man methodically turned the pages, compared the photograph with the live Krass and held a stamped page up to the light. Rhett glanced across and noticed a faint watermark of a stylised eagle embedded in the page. Isis had been thorough!

The guard turned the page and began to read a hand-written note tucked inside. He flushed and handed it to Krass. "I won't need this note from your... err... lady friend, General."

"Thank you," Krass replied, took the note, folded and placed it in a top pocket. Again, Isis had been cleverly included it as a distraction.

The guard's eyes switched to Rhett. "And today's password phrase is, sergeant?" he asked.

"When spring arrives the snow retreats."

"Everything is correct."

The guard handed the papers to him, stepped back and saluted with the grotesque Nazi salute Rhett remembered from old war movies he had watched as a boy. Krass returned a perfect backward type salute over his shoulder.

"Drive slowly," he hissed to Rhett as the barrier was raised and they drove forward in low gear. "That other guard looks trigger happy."

"No, they've heading back to the guardhouse," Pars said. "They're laughing. That girlfriend letter did the trick I think, Krass."

"Males don't change over the generations, do they?" A voice filled Rhett's mind. Loretta had returned.

Rhett grinned and relaxed a little. Their first hurdle had been successfully passed.

*

Rhett drove the transporter down a spiral road and into a gigantic cavern. The place was crowded with men everywhere dressed in both army and navy uniforms as well as civilians in overalls driving around in tractor and trailers. Their own vehicle fitted in with the local traffic quite well.

As they had discussed in their original planning, Krass slipped out of his general's uniform to reveal overalls beneath. Now he looked like a mechanic, again not a lot different from the workers around. Even his age fitted in, as many of the workers were elderly men.

Loretta and Irene flew out and disappeared in the glow of the overhead floodlighting. They returned within seconds and hovered by Rhett.

"You'd better get off this road, Rhett," Loretta said. *"Once we're out of here we arrive in an open area. A hundred or more Nazi soldiers are lined up in a parade."*

"I think they hastily arranged it to welcome you, Krass," Irene added.

"Me?" Krass muttered.

"Well, General von Rothstein."

"I see," Krass muttered. "I could fool the two guards at the gate but I doubt if I could be a general in front of a whole parade ground."

Rhett cursed and pulled to a stop. The tractors ahead continued and no traffic followed them. For a moment they were alone. "Where does that narrow alleyway on the left go?" he asked.

"I'll check." Loretta flew out and returned a moment latter. *"Seems okay. It comes out near the back of the cavern. Ahead is a tunnel that goes deeper into the mountain. There's a railway track coming out of it."*

Rhett nodded. That was on the map Isis provided. Almost a kilometre further in were the atomic energy laboratories and assembly lines for the weapons. The bombs would be brought out on flat cars towed by small electric locomotives. This would be as good a spot to deposit their own weapon as near the wharf, their original intention.

His heart pounded when he thought their transporter would be too wide to fit down the alley. However, by driving at a snail's pace between the piles of supplies he fitted in with mere centimetres to spare. If something came the other way...

Their luck held for they reached the other end without incident. Rhett pulled out of the alley, turned left, parked beside the end of the stores and stopped. There was a view of the tunnel entrance ahead. When he took a small sphere out of a pocket and squeezed it the result, though anticipated, left him gasping.

The transporter and everything inside, including Krass and Pars, disappeared. He felt as if he was sitting in mid-air in front of the storage shelves.

"Shut your eyes," Krass said from beside him. "Everything is still here but is invisible."

A calloused hand reached out and took his own. The advice was good. Rhett closed his eyes, felt his way to the overhead trapdoor, climbed out and slid down to the ground where he bumped into someone.

"Watch it," Pars muttered.

"Sorry" Rhett whispered.

A moment later both men appeared before him and he could see his own limbs. The transporter was invisible, but he knew it was still parked there as solid as ever. If anyone walked by they'd crash straight into it.

"Got everything?' Krass whispered.

Rhett nodded. "All neatly secured in my trouser pockets. These military overalls are quite handy in that way." He glanced around and took a mental note of where the transporter was parked. If all went well, they wouldn't need to return but it would be foolish to lose a safe refuge if it was needed.

He glanced at his companions. Krass looked determined with his newly shaven jaw jutting out while Pars, though nervous also looked ready and capable.

"Come on," Rhett whispered and, followed by his two companions, stepped out and headed for the walkway beside the railway track. He glanced up and noticed an overhead light turn from red to green.

A train was coming!

*

CHAPTER EIGHTEEN

Shelley sat in the oval shaped sofa with Dee and Corwin tucked in on each side of her. This was no ordinary chair, though, but a sophisticated viewing device that showed three- dimensional scenes in every direction. The cameras were just a minute few of the nanocraft that Rhett and the others carried to the Norwegian fiord.

"Remember, this is merely a machine," Isis said as she was about to turn it on. "You are not there in real life or even as an identity. In an emergency you can contact Rhett or one of the others by telepathy but I advise that you merely observe."

The scene came into focus with noise everywhere and the view of Nazi soldiers dismissed from a parade. It zoomed into an angry German officer. Shelley understood every word but whether she had been given the ability to understand German or the words had been converted to English, she didn't know.

"What do you mean by saying that the general's car has disappeared, Lieutenant Nussbaum?" A major was almost shouting at his assistant.

"It entered the main tunnel but never arrived here, Major Pfaff. It could have turned into one of the alleys between the stores but they have been checked."

"It must be somewhere!"

"The only other possibility is that it drove down the ventilation tunnel to the lower laboratories."

"How could a vehicle fit?"

"There's room. The ventilation tunnel was originally built to provide access for construction trucks while the main tunnel was built. I have a squad inspecting it." The lieutenant frowned.

"Out with it, Nussbaum."

"There was one minor inconsistency at the main gate. The general's papers contained a personal letter from his mistress, a highly erotic document that the guards were laughing about."

"So!"

"The report has just come in. The woman who supposedly wrote the letter doesn't exist. The other movements of the general himself are very detailed but there is no mention of her..."

"I know of his career. He is a somewhat ruthless but highly efficient officer and one in the Fuhrer's inner circle. He could be just discrete about this affair."

Lieutenant Nussbaum shook his head. "There's something else, too. There are no photographs of him with the Fuhrer or at any of the general staff meetings. I checked further. There are none of him inspecting troops of the Africa Corps but he was supposedly one of the leading officers there. My research found not one photograph of the man."

Major Pfaff glowered. "And your conclusion?"

"He doesn't exist either."

"So we have an impostor here in the most heavily guarded base in Norway?"

The lieutenant nodded. "Shall I sound the general alarm, Sir?"

"No. If they don't know we're onto them they will be easier to trace. As well as that ventilation tunnel, where else could they go?"

"The catacombs. That is the natural cave that the base was built out of. If an enemy had a map they could reach just about any level without entering the main tunnels."

"You're very knowledgeable about this Nussbaum?"

"One of our Norwegian informers grew up in the area, Sir. As a child, his friends and he would often explore the upper caves. Apparently the mountainside is dotted with secret entrances."

"And he knows the ones adjacent to this cavern?"

"Yes."

"Get him and the security squad. We must find this general..."

*

"I underestimated them. For a primitive species they are surprisingly clever," Isis muttered. "I knew about the lack of photographs but didn't think it would matter as they had no computers or internet in those days."

"And the caves?" Shelley asked.

"I missed them, too. They'll need to be blocked but otherwise they will not hinder our plans. In fact, they'll provide a useful diversion."

"I'll warn Rhett."

"What is it, Shelley?" Rhett's voice shouted into her mind.

"They know the general is a fake..." Shelley told him all about the conversation she had overheard.

"And you can move your monitors around?"

"Yes. Many of the nanocraft have lens attached. Isis is monitoring them."

"And you're safe?"

"I'm not there Rhett, not even as an identity."

"Good. Keep me posted if anything else important is noticed." His voice

faded.

"Dad will be fine, Mum," Dee whispered and squeezed Shelley's hand.

*

The locomotive looked like a squashed down London tube train with a helmeted driver straddling it like a motorbike. The carriages behind consisted of seven flatbed units, each with an armed guard sitting on each corner. The loads themselves were more spectacular. The atomic bombs sat on long skids. Each was shaped like an ancient witch's cauldron, even down to their black colour and circular shape. They towered above the guards to about three metres in height and a similar diameter at their widest part. Several pipes and tubes protruded from the sides and a silver rod stuck out their front like a grotesque nose.

"That's the plunger." Rhett remembered a diagram Isis had shown him. "The bombardier pushes the rod in to arm it. There is also a timer that can set to any time up to forty minutes. This is so the bomb doesn't have to be activated until the bomber is beyond friendly territory."

Krass and Pars both stared at him with no understanding of what he had said. Of course, they came from a pre-industrial planet and the concept was beyond them.

"Heavily guarded," Krass whispered. "How do we get our own weapon close enough?"

"According to Isis, it doesn't matter. We are as close as we need to get. We activate the nanocraft and they'll automatically do the rest."

"I'm worried," Krass muttered as the train drew closer and they retreated into the shadows. "How can Isis destroy this base and those bombs if her inbuilt systems won't let her kill anything?"

Rhett shrugged for the same thoughts had gone through his mind.

"Stop gossiping and do something," Pars interrupted. "There are more soldiers coming to meet the train."

Rhett nodded. Isis's instructions were to shake the glass sphere he had in his pocket before smashing it onto something solid. Afterwards, they were to get back into a hidden area and activate a second cylinder he'd been given. When the top was screwed, the portal would open before them to escape through.

It sounded simple...

*

Shelley jumped in alarm when Loretta and Irene awoke simultaneously and sat up. She swung her chair around and stared at them. "Are you both okay?" she asked.

"We are," Loretta replied. "Rhett told us to return to our physical selves. It's just about all done down there."

"Is it?" Shelley replied. "Look at the scene I'm watching."

A siren wailed and solders ran everywhere. The train slowed and continued moving forward at a snail's pace while soldiers lined almost shoulder to shoulder on both sides of the track. She could not see Rhett or the others but did notice a small black cloud float up towards the ceiling. It increased in size and headed for the tunnel where the train had entered the cavern.

A loudspeaker spat out orders and twenty or more machineguns opened fire at the cloud. Tracer bullets curled through the air and half the floodlighting overhead shattered. The remaining tracer bullets ricocheted off the ceiling, walls and any solid object in the way.

"Rhett!" Shelley screamed.

"It's okay," his calm voice replied. *"We're all safe and back in the transporter. They've managed to blow out half the lights."*

"Get back here" Shelley managed to make her words calmer.

"Soon. We can't see much so can you give us an idea about what is happening?"

Shelley gulped and moved her eyes around. At various times her view changed as a different monitor switched in. It was disorientating at first until she learned to move her eyes slowly and found that if she blinked twice, she'd switch to another view. Three blinks returned her to the original position and a turn of her head moved her around. Also by lifting her eyebrows the vision rose to the ceiling.

Dee and Corwin saw exactly the same view as herself but their eyes were helpful for they noticed small details that she missed while trying to navigate. After circumnavigating the cavern, she took up a high central position where she could see most of the area by merely turning her head.

Several things were happening. The train continued forward and moved along a wharf where it halted, the firing stopped as quickly as it started and soldiers stood still awaiting orders. These were blasted out through a loudspeaker but the words were distorted and she couldn't understand them.

"The harbour, Mum," Dee said.

Shelley turned and saw a U-boat surface through a bubble of spray. This was followed almost immediately by a second submarine.

"They came out of the water?" Rhett asked.

"Yes."

"So the entrance is probably under the surface."

"I've no idea but can go and look."

She switched to another monitor and saw the entrance. It wasn't submerged but the roof was only a few metres above the water. On closer inspection, she noticed that right across the ceiling; white foam was being created at a pace so rapid that it appeared to be poured out. But this was upside down!

"The nanocraft are reproducing and linking together," Isis said from behind her. "It's like a honeycomb. Once they link, a liquid is excreted between them. This solidifies and a solid wall build up that is as tough as concrete. It is a little like a coral reef being built but is millions of times faster."

Already the wall extended a metre out from the ceiling and walls and moved along ten centimetres even as she watched. The speed of construction was also increasing as more nanocraft reproduced, until the white wall began dropping like a curtain.

"They don't like it," Corwin shouted as more machine guns as well as a cannon from the rear submarine opened fire at the steadily closing entrance. Again, the bullets did nothing except blow out more overhead lighting. A siren sounded and the other U-boat began to turn and submerge at the same time.

"It may just make it," Isis said. "There are no bombs aboard so it can't do any harm."

The U-boat disappeared and bubbling water showed its journey through the water. Shelley found something new. Her vision was not hindered by the water itself. Seconds later she was watching the U-boat moving beneath the waves and into the tunnel. It moved slowly forward, under the growing wall and stopped!

The conning tower could not fit. It dropped but hit the ocean floor, wriggled like a drowning whale and stopped... just as the wall reached the deck and slid around both sides. Within seconds, the U-boat was nothing more than a bulge in the solid wall.

Shelley felt ill as she communicated with Rhett.

"It's a war, Shelley," he replied. *"If it had got away with only one bomb thousands of people would have died."*

"People died in Japan in 1945 after atomic bombs were dropped."

"I know but that was history as we knew it. We must return to that situation."

"He's right," Isis said. "To try to change the war as Rhett's world led it, will only form more alternative worlds with unpredictable consequences. All wars are tragic, even if you're on the winning side."

"Can you go and see what the entrance we came in is like?" Rhett asked.

Shelley moved out of the water, beyond the panicking Nazis and into the tunnel. An area lit up to reveal gap like a half opened curtain in the otherwise completely sealed off tunnel. The sunlight from outside shone in.

"There is a problem," Isis said. "Tell Rhett, Krass and Pars to open the portal and get out of there immediately."

"I heard," Rhett said. *"Give us a couple of minutes."*

"You have been overridden," Isis announced in a voice that was too calm. She turned to Shelley. "Your image is soon to be projected above the main concourse. Please read them this message." A sheet of epaper was handed to Shelley.

"Why me?"

"Protocols. A human must make this announcement."

Shelley gulped and looked up. It felt as if she was standing at the end of the wharf with the soldiers below as small as dwarfs. In fact, she realised her image was over ten metres tall.

"Soldiers of the German army and navy," she read in perfect German. A murmur went though the cavern as hundreds of eyes turned her way. The murmur turned to silence and a searchlight from the remaining u-boat turned and shone directly at her. "We are members of the United Nations that superseded the League of Nations. Our intention in coming to your base was to stop you manufacturing and using atomic weapons to destroy allied cities. Your base is almost completely sealed off. Unfortunately, our weapon, a self-replicating concrete is too strong. As well as isolating this base it has applied pressure to the atomic weapons. The plunger of the third bomb has been forced down and your other safety devices overridden. In exactly eighteen minutes it will explode. If you do not wish to die, please make your way out the main entrance. The opening there will close in sixteen minutes so the atomic explosion is confined to the underground caves."

Shelley felt her stomach drop for the scene before her disappeared and was replaced by a scene of the Earth below as seen from their orbiting spacecraft.

"Rhett!" she screamed.

There was a hiss of moving air, a wooden door appeared before her, opened and a grinning Pars followed by Krass and Rhett, walked through. The brief noise and view of panic stricken soldiers and sailors running towards the entrance tunnel moved out of focus and was replaced by an outside view.

A sergeant was shouting and trying to establish some resemblance of order as soldiers and sailors poured out the entrance. They were waved on down the road in, more or less, three lines. Officers appeared and one stalked across to a parked staff car. Three more officers boarded and the Mercedes roared away with its horn blaring.

At exactly the time announced the entrance was sealed. Shelley didn't know whether everyone got out but suspected many didn't. Exactly two minutes later the entrance glowed a bright yellow, turned to white and bulged out like a balloon. The ground around began to shake, slowly at first and then with a force so powerful that the entire fiord vibrated in an earthquake.

Next, the noise began from far above as rocks and snow formed an avalanche that screamed down the mountainside. There was no time for anyone to move before this avalanche, now a wall of debris scores of metres high, thundered down. It missed the top of the road where most of the personnel were but there was total oblivion further along. The road, including the escaping Mercedes, was covered in a million tonnes of rock that continued on to splash into the ocean below.

The scene changed and, for a moment, Shelley had a view of white hot smoke and melting rock. She thought she saw a horizontal mushroom cloud form, just before the scene began to vibrate and became a blur of spinning grey. The accompanying roars cut out and silence reigned.

The scene changed to the computer simulation of the parallel worlds with the two alternatives. Shelley remembered the red represented their universe while the yellow line showed the universe after the Nazis won the war. This time, though it was the yellow line that broke up and disappeared.

"We did it," she gasped

There was a flicker and an old oaken door appeared that was ajar. Inside it, Shelley saw lonely grassland bathed in afternoon sunlight.

Isis's voice sounded formal. "My inbuilt ethics commands me to return each and every one of you to your home worlds. However, if you hurry, I can hold this portal open for a few moments. If you go together, you can decide on your own fates."

"Does this lead back to Pars' world where we had problems with the villagers?" Rhett asked.

"Don't argue. Just go!" Shelley shouted in almost a panic. She grabbed the children by their hands and almost pushed Rhett forward. "Come on," she shouted to the others. Making sure that at least her family was with her, she walked through the portal and into blazing hot sunlight.

"Friends come in handy," Krass whispered mere seconds later.

"Oh my stars," Shelley gasped. She looked around and saw that everyone was there, well all the humans…Rhett, Dee, Corwin, Pars, Krass, Loretta, Irene and Sarine and, of course, herself were standing in knee high grass. With a whish, the portal behind them vanished into nothingness. Obviously, their journey was meant to be only one way.

Staring at them with its head sideways and grass in his mouth was Zarleg, not the Clydesdale version but the tsintaosaurus from Krass's original world. Behind the obviously delighted creature and in the shade of towering trees, she could see the wagon with a donkey grazing nearby.

*

The wagon was filled with Krass's belongings but contained nothing that showed any evidence that any of the others had been there before. On closer examination Krass found other inconsistencies. After holding a conversation with Zarleg, not unlike the very first one Rhett had overheard him having when they first met, he said that they must have returned to this world at a time before he had found Loretta, Irene and Sarine.

"Just a wee while before I found them, I'd say," he said and gazed up a Zarleg. "You can't remember us having visited a lower monastery or seeing one high in the hills?'

Zarleg bent down close to the old man and grunted.

Krass nodded. "That's right," he said. "We'd heard rumours of a castle filled with humans and were going there to check it out, right Zarleg?"

The tsintaosaurus rolled his eyes as if to agree and that he'd already pointed that out.

"So that's where we should head," Shelley said.

"Why?" Rhett asked.

Shelley caught his eye. "Neither Dee or I have our earrings now, I see no sign of a portal but the monastery could still contain one."

"Perhaps the abbot is there," Dee said.

"And perhaps we've gone in a gigantic circle," Sarine said.

"What do you mean?" Rhett asked.

"Well, we could still arrive here as identities when Krass found us. If we find the monastery and go through the portal everything we've done could be repeated."

"No," Shelley responded. "If that was so, Krass would be here by himself and we'd be where we were originally at this point in time. We're together here, so that much has changed. I think Isis has selected the best place to send us so we remain together."

Rhett nodded. Shelley was probably correct but one more problem about this scenario worried him. Was this their final destination and would they be stuck in this world forever?

"That's why I suggested trying to find the monastery," Shelley said to him. "It could be the one way back to your world."

"But not yours?"

"That's my last choice," Shelley whispered. "Your world is the place I'd rather go, otherwise it will be better to stay here on this planet away from the raging wars, Loretta, Irene, Sarine and I were involved in."

Rhett smiled and hugged her. "Right, so we head towards the monastery to see if the portal is there?"

"I think so." Shelley kissed him and nodded. Their journey wasn't over but they were safe and together at the moment.

*

CHAPTER NINETEEN

Over the next week, the nine humans journeyed through deserted land without meeting a soul. Between themselves, though, there were small changes that Shelley noticed and that wasn't just Rhett who now wore a flourishing beard or Pars, who'd managed to grow an almost ginger fuzz. Perhaps they had been happening earlier but she'd failed to observe them. Though physically much the same Dee and Corwin had become more mature. Corwin was not the frightened little boy they'd rescued and Dee was developing into a young woman. Krass and Loretta had paired up, as had Pars and Irene. Only Sarine seemed alone but had to become everyone's firm friend.

"Don't you miss an adult companion?' Shelley asked on their eighth morning after their arrival. They were together washing clothes in a stream.

Sarine glanced up. "No, I have everyone as a friend. It is all I need at the moment." She stared out across the stream, turned as if to say something but hesitated.

"Go on." Shelley encouraged.

"I've listened to the others talk. Loretta and Irene both want to stay here with Krass. Anywhere Irene goes, Pars will follow so he'll stay here, too. So far it has been a safe world but I'm like you two."

"In what way?"

"It's too far back in time. I miss modern society. Oh I know you said Rhett's world is still pretty primitive but..." She picked up a small pebble and tossed it across the water.

"Of course you can," Shelley said.

Sarine smiled. "I never asked."

"You want to come with us if we ever find a way back to Rhett's world?"

Sarine nodded. "I won't be a burden."

"Of course you won't be but even if you were, it would not be a reason to stop you coming. You have every right to chose where you wish to go as any of us. Whatever decision you make will be respected by everyone."

Sarine smiled. "I know. I guess I am not used to making my own decision about things. In my world, I went from an authoritarian childhood onto similar schools and was just beginning to learn freedom at university when I was called up for military service. There, of course, we were expected to obey orders without question.

"You remember?"

Sarine gulped. "Not really. It just came to me. If I actually try to think back to my earlier life, I can't."

"It's like that for me, too. Perhaps as time goes by, we'll

remember more about our previous lives," Shelley whispered. "Anyway, the children would miss you if we ever get to Rhett's world. All of us except him will be aliens in a strange land anyway, won't we?."

Sarine nodded. "But we're used to that, aren't we?"

Shelley laughed. "I guess we are."

They chatted as the time slipped by. Only Pars' arrival interrupted their conversation. He carried a bow and arrow he had made over the last couple of days and grinned as he held up two dead rabbits.

"We need fresh meat," he said.

"Wonderful," Sarine replied.

Shelley, however, frowned. "This confirms something Rhett and Krass were discussing last night. This world must be Krass's original one for Zarleg and the wagon are there but its been altered. Rabbits would not have existed in Krass's reptilian world."

"So, will we could meet humans or girifa?" Pars asked.

"Possibly both," Shelley replied. "We'll have to be on full alert, though. Anybody we meet could be hostile."

Pars paled slightly. "There's something else," he said.

"What?" Shelley replied.

"It could have been a cloud but I'm sure I saw smoke in the distance."

"A grass or forest fire?" Sarine asked. "It's pretty dry here and fires can start naturally."

"No. The reason it caught my attention was that it appeared white and quite small, you know like camp fire smoke going straight up."

Shelley nodded. "Okay, we'll talk to the others about it." She smiled. "Rabbit stew will be a welcome addition to our diet. Thanks Pars."

The boy grinned. "Just trying to be a help," he whispered.

"Everyone is a help," Sarine added. "We make a great team."

*

Early the following morning they were on the move. It had been a dawn start and the children were still asleep when Zarleg started his steady walk forward. As usual, Krass had gone exploring with Pars and Rhett while Shelley took the first turn in the driver's seat. Not that there was much to do. Zarleg as a tsintaosaurus appeared to be more intelligent than the Clydesdale in the other world. He seemed to sense where to go and Shelley was almost asleep when he veered off into a shallow valley.

"Zarleg!" Shelley called and pulled on the reigns. "We're meant to be going straight ahead. Why are you turning?"

"Probably likes the look of the grass along there," Irene said. She climbed through from the wagon and sat down beside Shelley.

Zarleg slowed, turned his head and gave a low rumble.

"I'm sorry," Shelley replied. "Krass is the only one who understands you. He's gone off to spy out the land. It'll be okay. He'll probably be waiting for us as he usually does."

Zarleg, though, refused to return to the original trail. He rolled his eyes, growled and sat down on his back legs.

"Stubborn brute," Irene said.

"No, it's more than that." Shelley climbed down off the wagon, walked forward and gazed up at Zarleg whose head towered above her. "So you think we should go up this side valley?"

Zarleg glanced down and gave a murmuring sound that Shelley had often heard him using when he agreed with Krass.

"For how long?"

Zarleg flicked his tongue and lifted his head.

"Just a little way?"

Another murmur.

Loretta joined Shelley and stared at Zarleg. "You want us to go up there to hide, don't you?"

"Humph!"

"I see," Shelley replied. "Okay, we'll just go up until we're out of sight. We don't want to lose the men."

Zarleg stood up, waited until everyone was onboard the wagon and took off at almost a gallop.

Shelley just hung onto the reins and let him go. They rattled and bumped through short grass, over hard ground that left no wheel marks behind and followed the base of a low hill until the junction where the drama had started was out of sight. Zarleg slowed, turned his massive head as if he was searching around and stopped.

He sat down on all paws like a cat before a fire and wagged his tail slightly.

"Okay, we wait for Krass." Shelley turned to the others. "I think a couple of us should climb the hill and look back over the trail. I'll go."

"I'll come with you," Sarine said.

"But stay in sight," Loretta said. "We don't want to split up too much."

"Fair enough," Shelley replied. "If we wave with both hands we've seen something, one wave means everything seems clear. We'll be no more than fifteen minutes. Okay?"

"And if we give you a double wave, get straight back," Sarine added.

*

A few moments later Shelley and Sarine crawled up the final few metres of the hillside and into a thicket of small bushes. Through the lower branches they had an excellent view of the trail they would have been on if it wasn't for Zarleg.

"Oh my stars," Sarine gasped. "We would have gone straight into them."

Below them was a long wagon train that was the most unusual type Shelley had ever encountered. The thirty or more wagons were almost identical to Krass's one but were pulled by both retiles like Zarleg, draught horses like Zarleg in the other world or huge horned oxen. Even from a distance where she and Loretta peeped out between the foliage, the inhabitants were also different. Most wore old-fashioned clothes with the women in long dresses and the men, hats and coats of a bygone era. About half were human and the others the hairless reptilian girifa. A third species were different again. Unlike the girifa, the females had breasts but the species had silver skin with a blue tinge and scales not unlike fish. In contrast to the other conservatively dressed settlers both males and females only wore loincloths wrapped around their waists and dropping no further than a miniskirt.

"What are they?" Shelley asked.

"I've no idea," Sarine replied. "Perhaps they're the natural inhabitants of this planet."

"We'll send a signal back that something is there and watch for a while." Shelley waited as Sarine slid back down the hillside until she wouldn't be seen from the wagon train and gave a massive double wave. She came puffing back and squeezed in beside Shelley.

"The men are back. I think Rhett wants us to stay, As far as I could work out he's coming up." She screwed her nose up. "Krass is talking to Zarleg. You know what he does?"

Shelley grinned and nodded. "The wagon train appears to be moving along pretty slowly. They're only going at a walking pace."

"Yeah, they've got kids running around everywhere," Sarine said as she slid in beside Shelley and moved some leaves aside. "Looks like new settlers crossing the country."

"But three species?"

"Perhaps it is normal in this world." Shelley glanced back down their side of the hill. Rhett and both children were coming up. As they neared the thicket they dropped to all fours and crawled up under the trees.

"A large wagon train," Rhett said. "How do you feel about it, Dear?" he asked.

"We need to make a contact sometime. Our supplies are almost all gone."

"But your inner feeling?"

"I feel confident."

Rhett nodded. "Shall we go in together to meet them or would you like Krass and me to scout it out?"

"Go in together," Shelley said. "I'm sure it'll be okay."

Her heart raced but there was no upset stomach or any nagging doubts in her mind. In fact it felt as if it was how everything should be. Dee, who had waited for Corwin to catch up, crawled in beneath the branches and beside her. She stared down at the wagon train below where there were only humans and girifa in sight.

Dee frowned slightly and turned to Shelley. "How do you feel, Mum?" she asked.

"Fine. Why?"

"I don't. Something down there is wrong."

At that moment a male alien, wearing only his loincloth walked out from behind a wagon. Dee froze, colour drained from her cheeks and she began shaking.

"No!" She was obviously terrified as she glanced up at Shelley with her eyes like saucers "Fishminds! They use their minds to enslave any other species they come in contact with. Those aren't settlers down there, Mum. They're slaves!"

"You've met them before?" Rhett asked in a calm voice as he placed an arm around Dee's shoulders.

"We all did," Dee sobbed. "Don't you remember?"

"No," Shelley replied. "Was it when we were together as you grew up."

"Yes, the fishminds attacked our village and almost half the villagers just packed up and climbed into a transporter they used. We never saw them again."

"Not a wagon?' Rhett asked.

"No a hovercraft with no wheels. I remember it."

Shelley felt a strange lethargic feeling of peace fill her body. It was okay. They wanted her to come and join the wagon train. Her stupid little daughter was having another fantasy. She smiled and glanced down. The alien was looking straight up at her. My, what a muscular guy he was. Perhaps... She giggled at the erotic thoughts that went through her mind and went to stand up.

However, strong arms grabbed and pulled her back down so quickly, her chin hit the ground and pain shot through her body. For a second she realised that something was wrong as Rhett held her in a vice grip. No... it was fine. If they joined the wagon train all their troubles would be over. That nice alien guy wanted her to come to him...

"Let me go!" she screamed without even attempting to keep her voice down. "They're friends. They will feed and look after us. Everything will be fine."

She struggled but a worried looking Rhett stubbornly held her down. "Help me," he called to someone nearby.

Shelley turned and almost snarled. It was Sarine. The little tramp had seen this wonderful guy too and wanted him. The bitch wasn't that innocent little virgin she'd pretended to be. Probably she'd been sleeping around with everyone including Rhett. She yanked her right hand free and scratched him firmly down the cheek with her fingernails. He cursed, blood oozed out but she was still held firmly on the ground.

"I'm sorry Mum," Dee sobbed and reached across,

"Stop it!" Shelley howled as her daughter's fingers reached her neck. She felt the pinch and the ground around began to spin before she remembered no more.

*

"What happened?" Rhett whispered as Shelley flopped back, unconscious beneath him.

"I had to, Dad?" Dee sobbed. "It wasn't her. That fishmind must have taken control of her thoughts. I have to stop them before it happens to us all."

"No!" Rhett screamed as Dee purposely stepped forward out of the trees and stood up well within view of anybody looking up from the wagon train.

At the same time her hand brought out a necklace hanging around her neck that Rhett had never seen it before. At the end of a golden chain was a small circular disc about the size of a dollar coin.

"Don't Dad!" Dee turned and sort of waved at him. He found himself paralysed in a half standing position and could do nothing, not even talk. He could, though see everything that his daughter did.

"Fry in your own evil thoughts!" she screamed as she held her necklace up. The disc glowed and a ray of white light shot out. It hit the alien far below and he collapsed to the ground with his limbs and body going into convulsions and silent screams coming from his open mouth.

Two more aliens ran out and Dee turned her disc. Two more rays shot down the valley with the same result. Within moments, a dozen aliens lay writhing and trembling on the ground. Humans and girifa gathered in a circle and hid the victims from view. They appeared to be doing nothing except watch the aliens on the ground.

"They're confused," Dee whispered. "The mind links used to control them has been cut but it will take time for the humans and girifa to begin thinking for themselves. It's like awaking from a nightmare."

"She's right, Rhett," Sarine said. "We have that time to get away. The chances are the fishminds will awaken first and re-establish their control."

"You know of them, too?" Rhett gasped and found he had full control over his body again.

Sarine stared at him. "Only now. Before Dee acted I remembered nothing. Dee saved Shelley and probably all of us, Rhett."

"Twist the disc like Isis taught you, Dee," Corwin shouted. "We haven't got much time, only five minutes."

Dee nodded, looked out over the wagon train in search of more aliens. There were none so she stepped back and into Rhett's arms. "Mum will be fine but you will need to carry her through," she whispered.

"Through what, Sweetheart?"

Dee looked up as her fingers twisted the disc. An old fashioned oaken door materialised as if suspended from the branch of a nearby tree.

Rhett lifted Shelley in his arms while Sarine opened the door. He checked to see that Corwin and Dee were with him and staggered forward on limbs that felt like jelly. Sarine waited and held the door open as he carried Shelley through.

Once inside, there was a sort of fog that surrounded him, so thick he could see nobody. Words formed in his mind.

"This is Isis sending you a personal message, Rhett. None of the others are hearing it. Just think your reply to acknowledge that you are in contact."

"I am."

"The alternative worlds are settling into a permanent state which, once completed will be irreversible. The problem that I have to overcome is one that personally affects you and your family."

"Go on."

"This was not your family before Shelley arrived unannounced in your holiday home, was it?"

"No...but." Rhett felt his heart race and anger rise inside. After everything they'd gone through!

"Thank you. I can sense your apprehension and love. "

"Why are you asking?"

"The world that Shelley and the children and also, as it turns out, that from which Sarine, Loretta and Irene came from, will not exist in the new realm. Once everything becomes permanent, none of them will be able to return to their old world. Any attempt will alter the quantum continuum spectrum."

"Meaning?"

"Like the world where the Nazis won World War Two, it will be as if they never were."

"They won't exist?"

"you are correct."

"And if they come home with me?"

"They will continue to live but without memories of their earlier lives beyond what they already know."

"Why?"

"Because, in quantum physics that never had any."

"So why are you bothering to tell me all this?"

"Because, if you wish I can return just you to your Earth..."

"No!" Rhett almost screamed out loud. *"Why can't they all come home with me?"*

"You are not a rich man, Rhett. How will you manage?"

Rhett frowned. *"I'm sure we'll all work together. Compared with everything we've gone through our problems will be minor."*

"I'll see what I can do. Go in peace, my friend." Isis's voice faded

The fog cleared and he glanced around. Shelley was still in his arms and the children, along with Sarine were beside him. His heart raced in sheer excitement for the sun shone in a window where the curtains weren't completely pulled across. Outside, he could see a line of blue ocean and waves tumbling in.

The portal had gone but they were all standing in the kitchen of his Riversdale holiday home back on Earth.

*

CHAPTER TWENTY

In the middle of the tears, hugs and outpourings of emotional relief, a mobile phone chirped. Rhett searched around and found it was his phone that was sitting on the ledge above the sink.

"Hello," he said.

"Mr Rhett Pennant, principal trustee of The Portal Trust?"

Rhett had never heard of the trust mentioned but the memory of Isis's last words made him hesitate.

"Err... yes. This is Rhett Pennant speaking."

"This is Gary Logan from Ryan and Logan Solicitors in Masterton speaking. You'll be pleased to know the tender your trust put in for the old Starkwell School property, buildings and school house has been successful. I've emailed the details to you."

Rhett's mind was in a whirl. "Why, thank you," he whispered.

"The finance has come through from the trust's bank account so all we require is your signature and that of one of the other trustees for the property to be yours."

"Which other trustee?" Rhett blurted out.

"Oh, any of the seven adult members can sign. As you know, your two children are equal trustees but your wife and yourself have power of attorney over them until their eighteenth birthdays."

"And how are my family listed?" Rhett's mind went back to his deceased wife, Lesley.

He heard papers being shuffled.

"Mrs Shelley Pennant, daughter Dee Pennant aged 12 at this date and her younger brother Corwin Pennant. Why, is there a problem?"

"Not at all. I'm just checking that their names are correct..." He wanted to ask more but decided it might arouse suspicion if he appeared to be too ignorant. "Can we come in today?"

"Yes. Any time before five will do. It'll only take a few moments. It's a pleasure working for your trust. Goodbye."

Rhett placed the phone down, turned to Shelley and repeated the conversation he had. "Mrs Pennant, it appears we are legally married."

It was Dee, though who flushed a bright red.

"And what do know about this, Young Lady," he whispered an almost a harsh voice.

Dee's lips trembled.

"It's okay, Sweetheart," Rhett lightened his voice and wrapped his arms around his daughter.

"Isis spoke to me when we were in the portal, Dad. I told her that I want us to be a proper family." She burst into tears.

"Rhett," Shelley retorted and took Dee into her own arms. "We are a family, Sweetheart. We always were."

"And did Isis speak to you?" Rhett stared at Shelley.

"Briefly," Shelley admitted.

"And..."

"Wanted to know if I wanted to come here."

"And you did?"

Shelley grinned. "I'm here, aren't I?" She reached up and kissed him. "Better check up on this lawyer..."

Rhett found his computer exactly where he'd left it and glanced at the date when the screen lit up. It showed only one day later than when they'd originally left through the portal.

"Time playing tricks on us again?" Shelley asked, She stood watching with the others as Rhett opened the email attachment from the lawyer.

The formal legal document showed a small sub-paragraph where the trustees of The Portal Trust were listed. As well as Rhett and his family, it included the full names of Sarine, Krass, Loretta, Irene and Pars as trustees.

"I'm with you but the others aren't on this world," Sarine said.

"Perhaps Isis did this just in case they came here sometime," Shelley suggested.

"She did, Mum," Corwin piped up.

"Corwin," Dee snapped. "We promised Isis we wouldn't say anything..."

"Sorry Dee." Corwin looked downcast until Dee grabbed him in a hug.

"It doesn't matter now that we're safe," she whispered.

"But the others aren't," Shelley said.

Dee glanced up. "They'll be okay Mum. Isis gave Krass a necklace, too."

*

After visiting the lawyers and the inevitable visits to shops for food, clothes and other items on which to start their new lives, everyone climbed into Rhett's Toyota. They headed out towards the old Starkwell School that, according to map Shelley pulled out of the glovebox, was twelve kilometres south east of Masterton.

They turned off the highway onto a narrow but good quality road that curved over prosperous rolling farmland parched in the summer drought.

"Almost there," Shelley said a few moments later. "It should be over the next rise."

"Dad, look!" Dee screamed and grabbed his shoulder from behind.

They'd just come around the bend and there, ambling along the left verge was a wagon pulled by a massive Clydesdale.

"Looks like our wagon..." Shelley began. "Oh my stars... it is our wagon!"

Sitting on the backboard was a blonde woman shading her eyes from the afternoon sun. She held a lead to a donkey that trotted along behind the wagon.

"It's Loretta!" Dee screamed. "Stop, Dad! It's Loretta."

But Rhett had already passed the wagon and pulled to the side of the road. He jumped out and stood overwhelmed as Loretta, Irene and Pars came running up to them. Sitting in the driver's seat, he could see Krass with a smile across his craggy face.

"But how?" he asked after another emotional meeting.

"We didn't like the primitive life so decided to try your world," Loretta explained.

"But it's only a few hours," Shelley said.

"What about the fishminds?" Dee added.

"Questions, questions!" Loretta laughed. "Tell them, Irene."

"It's been two months since you went up that hill and through the portal," Irene said.

"Your necklace was one powerful weapon," Pars interrupted with his eyes on Dee. "Completely sizzled the aliens."

"What?" Dee responded.

"They all died," Pars explained.

"The settlers were under their influence. It took them a week or more to come right and we travelled with them for another six weeks before we came to a small town. They got supplies and continued on west. We decided to stay in the town but didn't really like the place. Two hundred year old attitudes and the lack of even the most basic medical facilities helped to make our minds up," Loretta added.

"Krass used his necklace to open a portal," Pars continued "We arrived on this sealed road in hot sunlight with Zarleg back as a Clydesdale."

Krass drove the wagon closer, climbed down and glanced around at them all. "What a grand sight you are for tired old eyes. I should have guessed you'd be here waiting for us. This is your world, Rhett?"

"It is."

"When you left through that portal I told him we would meet you again." Loretta placed her arm through Krass's. "And don't listen to him about being old and tired,"

Zarleg whinnied.

"He doesn't like being a horse," Krass muttered in an effort to change the topic. He turned to the Clydesdale "It's either that or staying in that frontier town, old fellow," he said.

"And how long have you been here?" Shelley asked.

"Only about an hour," Loretta replied. "We were wondering where to go when you arrived."

"So where do we go?" Krass emphasised the 'do' as he raised his eyebrows.

"Home," Shelley replied. "It's just over the hill ahead."

She was right.

With the children left behind to ride in the wagon, Rhett and Shelley drove ahead and down into a shallow valley where a small wooden school, out buildings and quite modern schoolhouse stood. The hedges and lawns needed cutting, the garden weeding, the swimming pool was empty and grass grew through cracks in the tennis court.

However, the sign outside told them everything.

Over the 'For Sale' sign was plastered a bright yellow sticker with black letters that read 'Sold'.

"Oh Rhett, it's wonderful," Shelley whispered. She was almost in tears as she plastered an emotional kiss on his cheek.

The End